KT-560-456

STAFFORDSHIRE LIBRARIES
3 8014 04510 5928

FUGITIVE RUN

David West is a fugitive on the run, despite his innocence. He leaves Boston and heads for Junction Springs, Colorado. Here he meets detective Susan Kramer, who needs him to help discover the identity of her father's killer. When, eventually, the killer is nailed and brought to trial, West returns to Boston with his new expertise determined to seek justice and catch the man who killed his fiancée. Can West avenge her death and once more find love?

Books by Chet Cunningham
in the Linford Western Library:

JIM STEEL NO.5: GOLD TRAIN
WADE'S WAR

CHET CUNNINGHAM

FUGITIVE RUN

Complete and Unabridged

LINFORD
Leicester

First published in Great Britain in 2012 by
Robert Hale Limited
London

First Linford Edition
published 2013
by arrangement with
Robert Hale Limited
London

A catalogue record for this book is available from the British Library.

ISBN 978–1–4448–1704–1

Published by
F. A. Thorpe (Publishing)
Anstey, Leicestershire

Set by Words & Graphics Ltd.
Anstey, Leicestershire
Printed and bound in Great Britain by
T. J. International Ltd., Padstow, Cornwall

This book is printed on acid-free paper

Prologue

Junction Springs, Colorado,
25 June, 1895

David West's shoulder hurt as if a locomotive had roared through the fleshy part leaving a charred and bloody track where the steam had seared his flesh to the bone. Blood ran down to his elbow where it dripped off inside his shirt. Soon it would soak through and puddle on the ground in this outback canyon uphill from Junction Springs. West scowled when he realized he could smell the coppery scent of his own blood.

The sun bore down like an open hearth and he flicked drops of sweat off his nose and out of his eyes. It had to be 110 degrees where he lay in the dirt.

A robin musically marked his territory somewhere up the canyon. A soft breeze ruffled West's dark hair and cooled his burning cheeks. Each new surge of air brought the stench of his own sweat. Much of the sweat came from fear.

He shifted his weight where he lay on his stomach near a fallen ponderosa pine log he had dropped behind when the shooting started. This had been a simple information-gathering trip. A hand written note in his box at the hotel said if he wanted to know more about the Charlie Kramer death, he should go out to this small canyon in back of a deserted mine called Hannah's Hades.

Without a second thought he'd rented a red horse and ridden the four miles out of town and up the canyon. The directions had been easy to follow. His only precaution had been to buy a rifle and a box of cartridges at the Pallow hardware store before he left. The new six-gun on his right hip would be no help at this distance.

Now he knew he'd pulled a stupid,

dumb, greenhorn trick and it could cost him his life in a heartbeat. The two assassins had been over anxious and fired too quickly. One round missed, the second hit his horse. The third plowed through the fleshy part of his left shoulder and blasted him off his mount. He hit hard and rolled on the rocky ground, then dove behind the only protection around, this old log.

Now the odds were better but still one hundred to one that he'd never see the civilized pleasures of Boston again. Somebody wanted him dead and had hired two men to do the job. He walked right into their trap. This was all new to him, nothing like the polite society of Boston. An angry hot lead slug whispered over the top of the three-foot-thick log that shielded him. The rifle he held was the best he could buy in the small town below, an 1866 Winchester with lever action and firing .45–.70 cartridges. A favorite out West the clerk told him. Nine rounds fit in the long magazine and it had been full when he started on this exercise in stupidity. So far he hadn't fired a shot.

The two riflemen had well concealed firing positions less than fifty yards across the canyon and slightly above him. He lay near the left side of the ravine with a fifty-foot high rocky cliff behind him. On the top, it supported a smattering of new-green quaking aspen and a few ponderosa. He wasn't going to lay there and get himself shot again. The pain in his shoulder pounded like a railroad engine. For a moment he felt lightheaded, and then he steadied. He could barely move his left arm. He had no idea how serious his wound was.

There had to be a whole lot more to the mystery of Charlie Kramer's murder than he thought. It involved more than a sudden flare of anger or an old debt. It could be a planned act of revenge. Now two men were out to kill him and he wasn't sure why. The only reason was his work as a detective on the Charlie Kramer murder case.

Another pair of rifle shots blasted

into the silent Colorado mountain air just over the 6,400-foot level. One of the heavy slugs pounded into the pine log protecting him. The second nipped a splinter off the log two inches above his head and whined away into the red rocks behind him. The spent round loosened a trickle of dirt and small stones.

Another rock clattered down the bluff to the rear. He rolled over to his back, the rifle up. He saw a man fifty feet above pointing a rifle at him. Now there were three of them trying to kill him. The odds were getting worse. Much the way he had done on the shooting range back in Boston, West lifted the rifle and with the instant eye-hand coordination of a champion moving target shooter, he pointed and fired before his brain told him what to do. His shot came a second before the one from the man above. The .45-70 round blasted into the shooter. The wounded gunman's rifle went off as he fell but the round slammed into the rocks at his own feet. West thought he saw the gunman jolt to the rear as if hit in the chest by the round. He couldn't be sure. If the bullet had hit the bushwhacker, the man would no longer be a serious threat. He realized from habit that he had used his left hand and arm to fire the rifle. Now it hurt like fire when he moved it. He was thankful that his left arm hadn't gone dead.

Ten minutes ago, he had lost his hat when he dove behind this log. Now he pulled it toward him and edged the crown over the top of the ponderosa trunk. Two rifle rounds from across the canyon spun the hat out of his hand and slammed it ten feet away in the reddish rocks. The crimson boulders reminded him of blood and the large amount that he lost every minute from his wounded shoulder. The pain came again, boiling through him like the wild Atlantic surf in a winter storm. He gritted white teeth and beat down the urge to scream. When the worst of it passed, he tried to think how to get away.

There were two hidden men across the way with accurate fire aimed at him. One gunman was still behind and above him on the red rock cliff but almost surely badly wounded. No cover or protection either way beyond the fifteen foot log for forty or fifty feet up or down the narrow canyon. It would be a risk to run for the pines below. It was only three in the afternoon. This far north the sun wouldn't set until eight. Five hours to darkness.

The rifle fire came again; the shots spaced at irregular intervals of ten to fifteen seconds as if the killers had turned it into a game and took turns. Then they changed tactics and both weapons fired into the rocks on the steep cliff above him. Each round disturbed the face of the cliff. A few rocks rolled down then more. A boulder two feet in diameter broke loose and jolted down the cliff. It gouged out a torrent of rocks and dirt. In seconds the cascading stones and dirt loosened tons of the decomposing red strata. It had long been strained and cracked by freezing water in the winter and baking sun in the summer. It looked to David West as if half the cliff had broken off and hurtled downward at him.

He had to move or be crushed to death by tons of red rocks and dirt. If he ran he risked being shot to death by the two riflemen. He had no choice. David West rolled to his stomach, lifted the rifle with his good right hand, surged to his feet and charged on a zig-zag course toward a cluster of ponderosa pines fifty feet downhill along the side of the rock-strewn canyon. He stared straight ahead at his refuge as his new boots pounded the ground and every muscle in his body strained. He held his breath waiting for a slug from one of the high powered rifles to jolt into his body and slam him straight into the afterlife.

1

Junction Springs, Colorado,
24 June, 1895

A young man in a Western hat sat in a wooden captain's chair tipped back against the wall of the Pallow hardware store so only the rear legs rested on the boardwalk and the back braced the wall. The sun pounded down on him like a blast from a smithy's forge.

He wore a new brown hat with broad brim and low crown. He lifted it, wiped a line of sweat off his brow, then pulled the hat down until he could just see from under the felt.

He folded his hands on his belt buckle and sighed. It had been a long trip from Boston. He thought back over the past four days and marveled at how far he had come. He even had a different name.

His new name seemed natural enough. He had a cousin, David, and since he had moved west that seemed right as his last name. By putting the two names together he became David West. He liked the sound of it. At least with a name change he should be safe from anyone from Boston looking for Douglas Johnson.

He thought back to that terrible day two weeks ago when the police told him that the girl he had hoped to marry had been murdered. Then the police accused him of the crime.

Run. Fugitive Run.

It hadn't been all that hard to get away. The banks were still open and he had his ring of keys in his pocket. One of them fitted his Commonwealth Bank safe deposit box. He'd long had a nest egg stashed there, an ace in the hole for emergencies. No one else knew about it.

In the box he had placed a thousand dollars worth of bearer bonds, the kind that didn't pay interest or dividends, but also were not registered with anyone and were as good as cash. He had also secreted away in the box three hundred dollars in $20 greenbacks.

An hour and a half after he dropped out of his bathroom window becoming a fugitive, he had been to the bank, bought a hat that set low shadowing his face, purchased a suitcase and a few clothes and boarded the 6:15 train for New York.

Once out of Boston and with his resources, it had been easy to go from one train and restaurant to another and to a hotel then back on the train until he landed in Denver, Colorado three days later. He took a hotel room, signed in as David West and began planning his new life. There was no chance he could go back home to find out who had killed Jane and prove his innocence until the storm of newspaper stories and yellow journalism died down.

So, what did he do with his life? He couldn't get work in Denver in a stock brokerage house. He knew some big brokers might be checking fingerprints to be careful who they hired. Even without a check, somehow the word might get back to Boston that he was in Denver. He couldn't risk taking a job in a brokerage house under any name.

What did that leave? He had thought about it on the train. He had as his first priority to return to Boston and discover the man who killed Jane. Just thinking about her death now tore at his insides. He gasped then took a deep breath until the surge of anger and hatred for the killer passed.

The trouble was he was not a Pinkerton detective. So he had to learn how to be a detective. Learn by doing.

David looked up and down the small town's street. He had left Denver yesterday. It felt too large and probably had too good a police force. He found this village after a three hour train ride due south. They called it Junction Springs and he guessed it had about 8,000 people. He read the signs on the stores trying to pick out a new profession or at last a place he could get a job: hardware, real estate, women's apparel, general store, meat market, tinsmith, lawyer, saloon, gambling hall, more saloons, and a land office. Nothing struck a chord with him.

He had enough money to last him for a while. But a man had to have something to do. He had always had a job ever since he graduated from Harvard. He loved the stock market, but that was not a possibility.

He looked the other way and saw a sign: 'Kramer Detective Agency'. Yes, learn by doing. Maybe he could get a job there as an apprentice detective and learn the methods and routines and practices of being a detective. Then when he went back to Boston he would be ready to find Jane's killer. This time he had not flinched when he thought about Jane's killer. The pain was still there, but he was learning how to live with the fact of her death. Now he had to extract his vengeance.

He left the chair and walked across

the dirt street. A rider on a gray horse galloped through just in front of him and set up a rolling cloud of dust. He held his breath and hurried through the roiled air to the boardwalk.

As he approached the Kramer Detective Agency, he looked up at the door and almost at once crashed into a large man. West stumbled toward the building's doorway, tried to catch himself, then jolted into a figure that came out of the detective agency. He turned, lost his balance, and waved his arms. He sensed the other person falling as he went down on the boardwalk.

After the first quick shock of falling, he realized he lay on top of the person and rolled to one side. Then he saw a startled young woman's face staring up at him. She lay flat on her back on the boardwalk.

'Oh, miss, I'm sorry, I didn't mean . . . '

'Most people just stop a girl and say, Hello I'd like to meet you. This seems a little extreme, even for an easterner, don't you think?'

West scrambled to his knees and lifted the woman to a sitting position, then stood and helped her to her feet. He brushed himself off and watched her.

She was shorter than he by half a head, reddish-brown hair covered her forehead with a froth of soft curls and the rest had been stylishly piled high on top of her head. Her flashing green eyes watched him frankly curious.

'I'm sorry. I lost my balance. I couldn't stop. I didn't see you coming. I — '

She held up a slender hand with manicured nails and just a touch of pink polish.

'Enough,' she said, her grin widening. 'I agree it was an accident. I turned to look behind me, so at least half the blame is mine.'

She stopped talking and watched him. He stared at her. Slender, with high cheek bones, soft unblemished skin, reddish hair, dazzling eyes, a straight no-nonsense nose, and a full mouth. He'd seen flashes of perfectly even white teeth.

She brushed off her skirt. 'So, like two wild creatures, I guess we've sized each other up long enough. What do you think of me?'

Her remark surprised and flustered him. Here he had just made a spectacle of himself and now this pretty girl was talking bold as blazes.

'What do I think? You're terribly direct, aren't you? I think you're a beautiful young lady, pert and delightful. Sorry about the collision. My fault entirely.'

She smiled. 'You might at least offer to treat me to a cup of coffee or an ice cream to make up for your awkwardness.'

He frowned, dusted off his pants and nodded. 'Yes, my manners. Could I interest you in an ice cream?'

A smile darted across her face and she looked up at him. 'The fact is I'd love an ice cream. You're from the East, aren't you?'

'Well . . . yes. What gave me away?'

'First, your accent. It's not as broad as I've heard, but we have a few people here from Boston and New York. Your accent will give you away every time unless you work at losing it. Then there's your britches. You have on a brand new cowboy hat, and a range rider's blue shirt, which are both fine. The trouble is you're wearing a pair of fifteen dollar fancy eastern wool trousers. That's half a month's pay for a working man out here in Colorado. No regular cowboy would be caught afoot in the mountains in a pair of expensive pants like those. Then your shoes. They're strictly towner types. You'll have to get some cowboy boots and a pair of proper jeans if you want to pass as a native here in Junction Springs.'

David West chuckled in spite of himself. 'You figured out all that just by bumping into me and looking at me for a minute or two?'

'That's my business. What's yours?'

He remembered his plan. 'I'm a

detective. Figured this would be a good place to start up a new agency.'

She shot a quick glance at him. A small frown tinged her face and she pointed down the street toward the Grossamer Hotel where he stayed.

'They have ice cream at the hotel,' she said.

'Good, my pleasure.'

She watched him as they moved down the boardwalk in the warm afternoon sunshine. 'You say you're a detective. You worked as a gumshoe back east?'

He looked at her, puzzled a moment. 'Oh, yes, I've heard that term. We don't use it much in New York. A gumshoe, a detective because we wear soft soles so we can sneak up on people. Yes. I worked for a couple of firms, but decided I wanted to come west.'

'You probably got this far and ran out of money.' She piloted them into the dirt street aiming for the hotel. They had to wait for a rushing team of blacks pulling a farm wagon. Inside were four kids staring at the 'town folks'.

'Tell me, just why did you stop here at Junction Springs?'

'Looks like a nice little town, why not stop?'

They walked inside the hotel and past the desk to the dining room. She nodded at the head waiter.

'Jonas, a table please. We want some of your fine ice cream dessert.'

'Good to have you here any time, Miss Susan. Right this way.'

'Susan', he said to himself. He'd remember her name. Why did he say he was a detective? They sat at a window table with a view of the street.

'You never did tell me why you picked Junction Springs to settle down in.'

'Not sure I'll stay here. Still looking around. I've only been in town one day.'

'Right over there is the Kramer Detective Agency,' she said pointing out the window at the sign. 'Maybe you could get a job there. I hear they need a good detective.'

'Oh?' He lifted his brows, paused while a waitress came, and took their order for ice cream.

Susan frowned at him. She had small crinkle lines at the corners of her eyes and one dimple dented her right cheek when she grinned. Her attractive face was set off by green eyes.

'You're staring,' she said.

'Oh, sorry. It's just that . . . ' he took a quick breath. 'Just that I don't run into a pretty lady like you all that often.'

'Well, how nice of you to say so. Thank you. But you didn't answer me when I said the Kramer Detective Agency might be needing some help.'

He looked out at the sign and shrugged. 'Actually I don't know anything about them. How long have they been in town? What kind of clients do they have? How much do they pay? Is it dangerous work? Lots of things to consider.'

'You sound either like the cautious type or you really don't want a job,' she said.

The ice cream came and they both worked on it. West noted with surprise that the dish contained three flavors, strawberry, chocolate and vanilla. Interesting.

They didn't talk for a while as they ate, then she pointed her spoon at him. 'I see you aren't wearing a six-gun. You have anything against guns?'

'No, just didn't need one back east.'

'Back in New York?'

'Not in any of the big cities.'

'If you work for that detective agency, you'll need one and will have to be able to use it.' She smiled. 'Actually, I know the people who run the Kramer Detective Agency. I could introduce you to them . . . if I knew your name.' She held out her hand. 'I'm Susan.'

He took her hand. 'My name is David West. You have just one name?'

'For now. Maybe I don't trust you enough to tell you my last name.'

'Fair enough.' He smiled. 'OK, would you please introduce me to the

Kramers? I'd like to apply for a job over there.'

She took a spoonful of ice cream, looked at it a moment, then put the ice cream in her mouth. Susan shook her head.

'I'm not sure if I should take you to them. You don't sound like a detective. You ever work for Pinkerton?'

'No.'

'You don't wear a gun.'

'I could, I just don't need one right now.'

'How many cases have you solved?'

'Dozens, I've lost track.'

She watched him as they finished the ice cream. At last she nodded.

'All right, Mr Detective David West. Let's go see the people at the Kramer Detective Agency.'

He paid the tab and they walked across the street to the store front. He looked back the way they had come at a horse that shrieked in pain. When he turned back she had pushed the detective agency door open.

‘Here we are,’ Susan said. ‘It doesn’t look like anyone is in the front office.’

‘I can wait. I’m in no hurry.’

Susan smiled, moved behind the desk on the left, sat down and looked at some papers that lay there.

‘Should you be doing that?’ he asked.

‘Why not? My name is Susan Kramer. I own the Kramer Detective Agency. Now, do you want to apply for a job here, or don’t you, Mr West?’

‘What? You’re joking. Women don’t run detective agencies. Man’s work. I’ve never heard of a woman running — ’ He squinted a little and stared at her. ‘You’re not joking.’ David West closed his eyes and shook his head. ‘Oh boy,’ he said in a whisper. ‘Put my foot right in the middle of it, didn’t I?’

‘You did. A brand new cow pie. You’ll never get all of it off your shoes. Did you knock me down on purpose, too?’

‘A stupid accident. I stumbled.’ His voice rose in protest.

‘I thought maybe you were that desperate to meet a girl.’

'Not so. I have no trouble meeting young ladies. But I can see plainly that you're the kind of girl who would lead a guy on and on just to get him to buy her an ice cream.'

They looked at each other sternly for a moment then both broke up laughing. When they settled down, West eased into the chair across the desk from Susan.

'How long have you been a detective, Susan?'

'Not long. I helped out my father when he ran the agency. Then he . . . he died three months ago and I inherited the business. I had done mostly letters and that sort of thing for him, kept the books. Dad bought me one of the new typewriters and I typed up his cases for him so I knew about most of them. The problem is I've never really been a working detective. I closed out some of the cases that Dad worked on but that's about all.'

West chuckled. 'Actually I was making up a story about my detective experience. I've never been a detective, either. I acted like a 16-year-old trying to impress a pretty girl with that yarn. Am I forgiven?'

She nodded. 'What a detective agency we'd have. The two most inexperienced gumshoes in this end of Colorado.'

West stood and leaned on his chair. 'The way I see it is that it can't be that hard being a detective. Let me try. All it takes is some imagination, some research, talking to people, observing them, and digging out the facts. That doesn't sound hard at all. I used to sell stocks and bonds. I had to do a lot of research, investigating companies, checking facts. I think I'll make a good detective.'

Susan looked at him, then frowned and stared at the ceiling. 'I don't have many clients. I can't afford to pay much.'

'I'll work the first two months for free. If we get some clients and if I can help you make some money, then we'll talk about paying me.'

'You'd do that?' Her brows went up and she looked at him with a new expression of wonder.

'Sure, I have some savings.'

She stared at him and turned her head a little to one side. 'Might be a possibility. First, why did you quit selling stocks and bonds? It sounds like a good way to get rich.'

'The truth?'

'The absolute truth.' Her green eyes demanded it.

'I had to quit. Somebody accused me of something. I didn't do it but they didn't give me time to prove it.'

'So are the police hunting you?'

'I didn't say that.'

'Did you kill somebody?'

'No, I didn't kill anyone. I'll tell you about it some day. For now, you'll just have to trust me.'

'How can I do that? I don't know anything about you.' She drew some lines on a piece of paper on her desk then scratched them out. 'You don't look dangerous. Are you dangerous? Will you kill me some dark and stormy night and run away with all of the money in the cash drawer . . . roughly a dollar and sixty-nine cents?'

'I'm about as dangerous as a cotton tail rabbit on the Fourth of July and I'm not short of money.'

'You said two months' trial run with no pay?' she asked.

'Make that three months with no pay.'

She stood and held out her hand. They shook. 'David West, welcome to the Kramer Detective Agency. I've even got a case for you to work on. My father died, but I didn't tell you why. Somebody murdered him here in the office late one night. No witnesses. Nobody saw anyone come in or go out of the office. The case is still open with the Bruno County district attorney's office.'

'Your father murdered? Why?'

'I have no idea. He must have had enemies. He was sheriff here for eight years. By the nature of the job, a sheriff always makes a lot of people angry. At least one was killing mad. He lived here a long time, over twenty-five years. Only two houses and one store here when he arrived.

'The district attorney investigated Daddy's death for a week then gave up. He said he could find no evidence of any kind. Evidently someone walked in the office and shot my father. The DA said it was probably someone Father knew and maybe trusted. No signs of a fight or scuffle were found.'

'You don't have something simpler for me to start on?'

She shook her head and blinked rapidly, but no tears showed. He knew how she felt. She was heartbroken, still grieving, angry, furious, but with not much she could do about it. He felt the same way about Jane's murder back in Boston.

West took a deep breath and pushed down his own sudden feeling of the loss of Jane.

'No, I don't have any other cases. I want . . . I *need* to know what happened to my father and I want to see the killer punished. That'll mean more to me than solving a thousand cases.'

West knew that feeling. He understood about the gnawing ache to find a killer. Just the way he had to find out who killed Jane Poindexter and see him punished. He'd do it one of these days. He'd go back to Boston and find that killer. But not yet. Not until he learned how to be a good detective.

'I understand, Susan. Oh, may I call you Susan or should it be Miss Kramer or just boss?'

She smiled and he liked the way the small lines deepened and a dimple showed for a moment under her green eyes. 'Susan will be fine.'

'Do you have a file on the case? Anything that the district attorney dug up?'

'What there is of it. Sheriff Ramsden made an inquiry. Didn't seem like he tried hard enough. The district attorney said he spent two weeks on it and came up empty. You might go talk to him.'

She handed West a folder. Inside he found three sheets of paper with pencil notations and a story from the newspaper. The story read stark and cold:

DETECTIVE KRAMER KILLED IN OFFICE

Charlie Kramer, pioneer resident and longtime lawman here and operator of the Kramer Detective Agency, died late Tuesday night of gunshot wounds to the back, according to Harbin Ramsden, Bruno County sheriff.

Deputy Sheriff Ken Lawton found Kramer slumped over his desk as the lawman made his regular rounds a little after 1.30 a.m. Kramer's outside office door stood open and two lamps burned on his desk. Kramer sat at his desk and reports show he was shot in the back three times at close range probably with a large caliber hand gun.

The sheriff's department has no suspects. The funeral was held on Friday from the Lutheran Church with burial in White Hope Cemetery.

Sheriff Ramsden said that an investigation continues on the case and District Attorney Marlon Ferris said his office would also conduct an investigation 'to find the perpetrator of this heinous crime'.

Kramer, well known around Bruno County, had been elected twice to four-year terms as sheriff, and later one two-year term in the Colorado house of representatives. He leaves a sister in Iowa, a brother in Maine and his daughter, Susan Kramer of Junction Springs. She said it was too soon for her to decide what to do about Kramer Detective Agency, where she had worked with her father.

Susan watched him read the newspaper clipping.

'Not much to show for a man's life, is it? He did a lot of good for this county, now nobody even wants to find out who shot him.' Susan took a deep breath. Her chin quivered a moment then steadied. She squared up her shoulders and blinked once, before her eyes showed firm and green.

'Well, Mr West, you'll need a desk. That one on the other side should do. My father used it. I cleaned it out a week ago. I'll find you some paper and pencils and maybe a file folder or two. Oh, can you type?'

'Yes.'

'Good, then I won't have to read your handwriting, no matter how good it is.'

They looked at each other then West grinned and tried out the chair behind the desk. He adjusted it a little and examined the drawers.

Susan put on his desk some pads of paper, a dozen unsharpened pencils, a small hand held sharpener, and a coffee cup.

'New cup, we used to keep it for visitors. We didn't get many. We have that pot-bellied wood stove toward the back to keep the place warm in the winter. If it doesn't get too hot in here in the summer we make coffee on the stove as well. Small supply of wood out back. Have to remember to get some more before the snow flies this fall. Anything else?'

'Yes. Would you type up a letter introducing me as a new member of your agency? Otherwise nobody will know me from your Uncle Pete's hound dog.'

'Good idea. You want it now?'

'Figured I have three hours of sunlight left. I might as well go pay a call on Sheriff Ramsden and see if he's come up with anything new in the past three months. Can't hurt.'

Susan sat at her desk and pulled the typewriter over. She rolled in a piece of Kramer Detective Agency stationery and started to type.

'West, I like the way you're getting started. This might just work out after all.'

He chuckled. She finished typing the short letter and gave it to him. He folded it and put it in his shirt pocket.

'Now, two more questions. Where is a good place to eat in town? Be choosy because my next question is may I take you to dinner tonight to celebrate my new found employment?'

'The Grossamer Hotel isn't bad. A lot of the locals like to eat at the Chef's Galley on Third Street a block this side of the railroad station. Dinner tonight? I'm trying to think up a good excuse, but I can't. I guess I owe it to my new employee to introduce him to some of the local people. Yes. Let's go at 5.30 before the rush.'

'Good. I'll meet you here about five. Now, point me in the direction of the sheriff's office. Don't I remember seeing a court house somewhere?'

Ten minutes later, West walked into

the Bruno County sheriff's office in the basement of the modest sized county building and asked to see Sheriff Ramsden.

A moment later, in an office to the side, the sheriff looked up from his desk and West liked him at once. He had the appearance of a grizzly bear, well over 200 pounds, and surely over six feet tall. His black hair bristled in a dozen directions refusing to lie down and jug handle ears stuck out like railroad signals. His eyes glowed a soft brown under bushy dark brows and he wore a full black and gray beard trimmed to a half inch length over his face and neck.

David West flinched slightly when he entered the lawman's office. It just felt dangerous knowing that there must be a warrant for his arrest back in Boston. He had no idea how far they might have sent notices about him. Would a little town like this care about a fugitive from Boston?

Sheriff Ramsden didn't rise. He held

out an oak branch of an arm and gripped West's hand forcefully.

'West, eh? Good name for a man out here.' He took the letter West gave him, read it, and handed it back. 'So you're helping out Susie over at the detective office. Shame old Charlie getting shot that way.'

'My first job is to find out who pulled the trigger and why he was murdered. Has anything turned up in the past three months?'

A flicker of a frown creased the sheriff's face but it vanished almost at once. 'Not item one on old Charlie.' He rubbed his chin. 'That accent, you got to be from New York. Heard a gent who talked exactly that way.'

'Guess I can't hide it, can I? Oh, could I see your file on the case just to get familiar with the facts?'

'Ain't got no file. We investigated for a week, couldn't find hide nor tail of a suspect or a motive. Gave what I had to the district attorney and closed out the case. Can't have a batch of problems like that cluttering up my files.'

'Then I can check with the DA for his files on the case?'

'Might be. Reckon he still has them. We both moved on to some other cases we have a chance of solving.'

'Fair enough. I'm at the Grossamer Hotel for now. If anything happens on the case, let me know.'

The sheriff waved and David West left the office. Something bothered him. Had the sheriff's attitude changed when he found out West would be working on the Kramer killing? Might just be West's suspicious nature. As a salesman he had learned to read people's expressions, their moods and emotions. Had there been a shift in the sheriff when they started talking about the Kramer case or was it only his own overactive imagination?

On his way to the district attorney's office, West made the same silent pledge that he had made the first day he found out that Jane had been murdered. 'No matter how long it takes, no matter what it costs me, I will do everything in my power to get back to Boston and dig out the monster who murdered Jane Poindexter.'

2

Boston, 23 June, 1895
Three days after Jane's murder.

J. Thurston Paine leaned on the desk and glared at Boston Police Captain Zimbelist. His blue eyes blazed with fury as he slammed his fist down on the polished wood.

'Captain, I don't give a hoot what your superiors said. You haven't done enough to recapture the man who killed Jane Poindexter. You let the killer slip through your policemen's guns.

'What are you doing right now to track down Douglas Johnson?' Paine undid the button on the blue velvet jacket allowing the purple scarf knotted at his throat to swing free.

Captain Zimbelist smiled wanly and tried desperately to hold his temper so he didn't backhand this young, mon-eyed imbecile.

'As the chief of police told your father this morning, Mr Paine, we're doing all we can. We have no information about Johnson at all since he slipped out of his bathroom window. He could be anywhere in town, out of town or on his way to San Francisco or even Alaska. We only have circumstantial evidence against him, you must realize. Nothing iron clad.'

'Not iron clad?' Paine shouted. 'You have his white linen scarf, the death weapon. He admitted it was his. He said he was at Jane's house after midnight the same night she died. You know he took her home after the ball. You know she would open the door or her ground floor window for him later after her parents slept. Oh, Johnson killed her all right and I'm going to prove it. If the police won't do anything about it, I'll have to roust him out myself.'

Paine closed his eyes in frustration,

stalked to the door and back, then fixed his angry stare on the policeman. 'Captain Zimbelist, the chief of police instructed you to co-operate with me in every way you could.'

'Yes sir, that's right.' The captain took a long breath and looked away. His eyes glistened in anger for a moment then he relaxed. 'Mr Paine, you can see everything we have on the case. Besides what you already know, we lifted his fingerprints from the red vase in the entranceway. This is something new for us, but we're getting good at it. One big problem we have is that nowhere in the victim's bedroom or on the window or window sill could we find any of Johnson's fingerprints. That would have been conclusive evidence.

'We also know that he did not withdraw any funds from his checking or savings accounts in his two banks. His stock and bond portfolio remains untouched in his father's brokerage house safe.'

'So, what's he doing for money?' Paine barked.

'I have no idea. It's our assumption that he's left Boston, which makes it that much harder for us to find him. He hasn't been seen by any of his friends or relatives here in the city. He hasn't been back to his apartment which is under twenty-four-hour watch front and back. He hasn't contacted the Poindexter family or been to the undertaker to view the body. That's partly why we assume he's left Boston.'

'You're pathetic. Make me a photograph of his fingerprints to take with me. I'll get pictures of him. It's only been three days since . . . since Jane died. A ticket seller at the train station might recognize a picture of Johnson. He would have bought his ticket in the afternoon. I'll contact them today. Have a copy of your files on the case and that fingerprint photo ready for me by four o'clock. I'll pick them up here.

'Now, I'm off to the train station.' He

glared at the captain once more. 'I'm determined to bring that killer to justice. Poor Jane is dead. It's the least I can do to honor her memory.'

Paine lifted his silver headed walking stick and scowled at the officer. He set his silk hat firmly on his head and stalked past Captain Zimbelist and out of the police station.

A short time later, the angry young socialite talked with the station master at the Union Railroad station in Boston.

'Yes, Mr Paine, we'll be glad to cooperate. The man working the window that afternoon for out of town tickets would have been Montgomery, Gerald Montgomery, one of our best. He's on duty now if you'd like to talk to him.'

Five minutes later the station master and Paine went into the back of the ticket counter area and another seller took over Montgomery's window.

After quick introductions, Paine spelled out the problem.

'We believe that the killer left Boston by train that same afternoon, three days ago. I know it's asking a lot, but do you remember any strange ticket requests on that day?'

Montgomery shook his head wearily. 'Mr Paine, I deal with two or three hundred customers a day. It's nearly impossible for me to remember a certain ticket buyer from three days ago.'

'Did you see the picture of Douglas Johnson in the newspaper the day it told about the murder of the pretty lady, Jane Poindexter?'

'Oh, sure, I read the article. A shame a pretty lady like her and so young. Yeah, a picture of a man ran with the story.'

'That's the one I'm hunting, Doug Johnson. He's five-ten and weighs a hundred and sixty-five pounds. Twenty-six years old, has brown hair, speaks well. He'd probably want a ticket for some distant city.'

The ticket seller frowned. 'I do

remember one young man who became rather agitated with me for not being able to write him a ticket all the way to Denver. I told him I could get him into New York City on our line then he'd have to arrange with another railroad for passage to any other city. He didn't get violent, but scolded me proper and said time was important to him. As I remember, he was young, in his twenties.'

'You said he wanted to go to Denver?'

'Yes, but I can't be sure that's the man you're hunting.'

Paine held out a photo of Johnson to the ticket seller. 'Take a look at this. That's Johnson. Is that the man you said was nervous and in a hurry three days ago?'

The railroad man squinted at the picture, took metal rimmed eyeglasses from his pocket, and put them on. 'Let me take a better look.' He stared at the picture, moved it away and then back. At last he smiled.

'See the spot right here under his eye? That could be a mole. The gent I sold a ticket to New York to had a mole the same place. If I was a betting man, I'd say that this is the same person I sold a ticket to New York to three days ago. The nervous one.'

The ticket seller frowned and looked at the picture again. 'Yep, now I remember his eyes. A little hooded. I've always wondered what causes that. That's the same guy as in the picture.'

Paine took the picture, thanked the railroad men and hurried out of the depot to catch a cab home. He had to pack. This could be his only clue to finding Johnson. A slim lead but the ticket seller had been positive the man was Johnson. Denver wasn't nearly as large as Boston or New York City. Boston had about a half million residents. Denver had less than 125,000. If Doug Johnson tried to hide in Denver, he'd find the killer.

Junction Springs, 24 June, 1895

When David West left the sheriff, he went to the first floor and found the district attorney's office. Inside a secretary asked his name and said she would tell Mr Ferris that he had a visitor. She vanished through a door to the left and came back a moment later.

'Mr Ferris will see you now.' She led him into the next office. 'Mr Ferris, this is David West.'

The DA stood from behind his desk and offered his hand. They shook. Ferris had short blond hair parted on the left, matched West for height, but showed at least twenty pounds overweight. Sweat beaded his forehead and he wiped it away with a white handkerchief.

They sat and West gave him the letter of introduction and told him about investigating Charlie Kramer's murder.

The DA's face showed a sudden concern. He nodded. 'Wish I could help you more than I can. I knew

Charlie for a long time. I've been in town fifteen years myself. We have a file on the case. Still open, of course. Sheriff didn't come up with much and Charlie's murder caught me right in the middle of a tough jury trial. My time was all used up.'

He nodded. 'Glad to have you here. My secretary will get the file for you on the case and copy anything you need from it. If there's anything else we can do, come see me.' They shook hands again and both went into the outer office.

The DA spoke to his secretary a moment, went back to his office, and closed the door. The girl looked in a file then brought West a folder.

West went through the material quickly. There were only four sheets of paper. He found the report of the first deputy sheriff on the murder scene and asked the girl to make him a copy.

A few minutes later she handed him the typewritten page, he thanked her and went outside and down to the street. The one page report wasn't much, but it was a start.

He thought about Jane Poindexter again. Every day since he had fled Boston he mourned her. She was the woman he would have married, a best friend, and a marvelous lady he adored. It would take him years to get over losing her. Even now he felt a catch in his throat as he thought of her that last night, so lovely, so delightful, and in love with him. He shook his head to come back to the present. He was more determined than ever to learn how to be a detective so he could go back to Boston and find the real killer.

West continued down the street to his hotel where he just had time to wash up and put on a clean shirt before he went to meet Susan.

She was at the office when he arrived. They went on to the Stagecoach Restaurant. They ordered and as they talked, he learned a lot about his new employer. She had lived in Junction Springs since birth twenty-two years ago and graduated from the twelfth grade. She studied one year at the Denver Normal School, but decided she wasn't that interested in becoming a grade school teacher. She wore no rings so he decided she wasn't married.

He enjoyed listening to her talk. Now and then her face lit up like a streak of sunshine on a cloudy day.

'After I came back from Denver I helped Dad out at the office. By then he had a new typewriter he hated to use. I learned to type. Turned out that I enjoyed working at the office. I loved watching and helping as Dad investigated a problem or a crime and dug out the real culprit. I never figured that one of them would come back and kill him some day.

'The sheriff said it was possible that the killer was one of the men Dad put in prison when he wore a sheriff's badge years ago. Dad never told me about anyone threatening him.'

She looked up quickly. 'Oh, I want you to carry a hand gun at all times.

Except when you're sleeping, of course. If you don't have one, I'll get one for you tomorrow from the Pallow hardware store.'

'Good idea,' West said. 'But I can afford to buy a six-gun. I might as well get a rifle, too. I've heard a lot about the Winchester 1886 repeating rifle with a nine round magazine. That sound all right?'

Sue shook her head. 'I know nothing about guns or rifles. I'm sure you'll get something to do the job. I just want you to be protected in case we uncover something that the killers don't like and they come after us . . . you . . . me.'

'You think somebody in town killed your father?'

'I've always thought so. Dad never worried about a convict coming back for revenge. He often said most of them knew they got what they deserved and were glad they weren't hanged. I had a feeling, though, that during the last week of his life he knew something he didn't tell me, something important. He never got around to confiding in me.'

West watched Sue eat. She did full justice to the rare half pound steak dinner with all the side dishes. Sue touched her upswept reddish brown hair and looked at him.

'You haven't told me anything about yourself. You speak like an eastern gentleman, probably raised in a good family. Are you from New York City?'

'North of there a ways.'

'I've always dreamed of going to New York on the train. Wouldn't that be an adventure? Are there really as many people in New York City as they say? I saw in the newspaper that there were almost three and a half million people there. Goodness, I'd think that they would be stepping all over each other.'

West chuckled. 'Actually people do tend to get in each other's way a little. They have dozens of laws about that but most people are working too hard to make a living to worry about bothering anyone else. On the whole, people get along well in the city. What about Denver? You said you went to school there. I hear that it's growing fast.'

'It is but it's not huge yet. But millions like in New York. I just can't imagine what that would be like.'

'One of these days I'll tell you. Now what about some ice cream for dessert with all sorts of syrups and red cherries and whipped cream piled on top? Back in New York they call it an ice cream sundae.'

'Why? This isn't Sunday.'

That made him laugh.

They ate the sundaes, then he walked her to her house three blocks from the center of town and only four from the office. The house loomed three stories over them at the front door and he figured it had fifteen rooms.

'Dad built it ten years ago. It's way too big for me. I'm thinking of selling it and buying something smaller.'

She touched his hand. 'I thank you for a delightful dinner, Mr West. Now don't be late your first full day of work.

We open promptly at eight o'clock.'

'Yes, ma'am, I'll be there, boss.' He grinned.

She smiled, went in and closed the door.

He strolled downtown and checked his pocket watch at the first saloon where pale yellow light splashed out a front window. Five minutes after seven. Maybe he'd stop by at one of the saloons and have a beer and see what talk he could hear. Taverns in Boston were always a good place to get the feel of the town. It must be the same here.

He ambled on down the street and turned into a saloon called the Golden Dragon.

As a drinking place, it didn't measure up to the fancy saloons in Boston. Plain wooden floor, bar along one side and a dozen tables for playing poker. At the far end a few tables for faro and other games of chance. He walked to the bar and ordered a beer, paid his ten cents and watched the locals. Not more than a dozen in the place and half of those in one poker game.

He watched it a while. A quarter limit game. Nobody was going to lose the ranch tonight. A girl came from the back near a curtained doorway. She had on a low cut dress that showed off her figure and a skirt that stopped just past her knees. She might have been pretty if it wasn't for too much rouge and lip color. Her henna red hair fell around her shoulders. She grinned.

'You're new in town. How do you like the scenery?' She twirled and her short skirt flared out a little.

'I've seen worse. How is business?'

'Slow tonight. Lots of time for you.'

'Sorry, I'm working. You remember Charlie Kramer, the ex-sheriff?'

Her forehead furrowed and she nodded. 'Sure. He's dead.'

'Who shot him?'

She frowned a moment then lifted her penciled in brows. 'Why ask me?'

'I'm asking everyone I talk to. Do you know?'

'No, but I hear it was somebody right here in town.'

'Man or a woman?'

'Woman? Now that's a thought. Charlie used to come see me once in a while. He had no wife. Woman? Yeah, a woman could have shot old Charlie.'

'You think on it.'

She nodded. 'Yeah, if I get time. I'm Lola.'

'Good. I'm David West.'

She hesitated, saw someone at the bar and moved over and put her arm through his and kissed him on the cheek.

West went back to the bar and signaled the apron who pushed a draft beer down the slick top of the bar and came along to collect his dime.

'You must have been in town a while,' West said. 'Who runs this village? Any one man call the shots, like the mayor, the sheriff, a big businessman?'

The barkeep chuckled. 'Not a chance. We got a city council and those guys think they run things. Maybe they do. The mayor isn't much; the sheriff used to sell boots and leather. We're not a town with a lot of powerful people.'

West grunted and sipped his beer. When the apron came past the next time, West asked him the question of the day: 'Who shot Charlie Kramer?'

The bar man said surprised, 'I don't know. The word was it had to be someone he knew and trusted. That could be half the people in town. Even the DA gave up on that one. You some kind of a detective or something?'

West finished his beer and nodded. 'Mostly something. Thanks.'

He walked out of the bar and stood for a moment looking down the street. Should he try another watering hole or call it a night? He had about decided to give the Laughing Lady saloon across the street a try when he felt something hard press into his back and a gruff voice sound close behind him.

'Easy now, friend. Don't make any quick moves or this hogleg will go off sudden like. Just do as you're told and you might live to see the sun come up in the morning.'

3

David West felt the object in his back and reacted at once. He put on a thick British accent and slowly raised his hands.

'I say old chap, you really must have the wrong man. I'm just in from Bristol, England, you know . . . '

He felt the gun in his back ease off the pressure for a fraction of a second and that's when he knew the gun wielder was not sure he had the right person. West doubled up his fist and did a spinning back blow with his right hand aimed at the man's head or throat.

His move was so fast that the gunman wasn't ready. West's fist landed squarely on the man's neck and pounded him to the side. West slashed his left hand down at the weapon hitting the man's wrist and jolting the six-gun out of his grasp.

The attacker wailed in pain and staggered back a step holding his right wrist. Then he surged to the side and ran down the street leaving his weapon on the boardwalk where it had fallen.

West picked up the revolver, hefted it, then pushed it in his belt, and decided he should get back to his hotel room. He frowned, wondering why someone would try to hold him up. Or was it more than just a robbery? He could have been kidnapped, held prisoner or even taken down a dark alley and killed. Why? Who even knew who he was or why he was in town?

He pondered those questions, but he knew part of the answer. In a place this size, half the people in town must know that he was a new arrival. He had talked about the Charlie Kramer murder case with six people. Could one of them have told someone about his questions and that person didn't want him to investigate the murder?

He mulled it all over on his way back

to the hotel. Once inside his room, he locked the door with the simple skeleton key. The thing was worthless. He took the wooden chair in the room and slid the back under the door handle bracing the back legs on the floor. If anyone tried to break in, he would cause a lot of racket.

At least the room had electric lights. One single bulb hung from the ceiling with a string for a switch.

He sat on the bed and took out a small pad he had brought from the office and wrote down what he had found out so far. Charlie must have known his killer. Two shots in the back of the head. No suspects. The DA not investigating. Somebody tried to hold up or kidnap West his first day in town.

With that down on paper, it seemed easier to think about the case. He unpacked his few belongings in the dresser. He'd buy more clothes tomorrow including some jeans and cowboy boots. Also he would check out the revolver he picked up from the attacker.

If he liked it, he'd use it. He needed some more rounds and somewhere to do some target practice to find out how the handgun fired.

He outlined tomorrow's work in his mind and then crawled on top of the lumpy mattress. West reached over and picked up the gunman's weapon from the floor and checked the loads. Five and the hammer on the empty. Good. He put the six-gun beside his pillow and went to sleep almost at once.

* * *

When he arrived at the Kramer Detective Agency the next morning promptly at five minutes until eight, he found the door locked. He left a note that he would be at the Junction Springs Record newspaper office and headed for the building that housed the town's only paper. He had spotted it on his way to breakfast.

A young man came out from the back room wiping ink off his hands. He had black smudges on his nose and one cheek, red hair cut close, and snapping green eyes. He wore a black printer's apron with a large pocket in front and grinned at West.

'Sir, how may I help you this fine morning?'

'Are you the editor?'

He grinned. 'Oh yes. Editor, typesetter, printer, devil, circulation manager, advertising director, and delivery boy all rolled into one. 'Tis a one man operation, when we operate.'

West held out his hand. 'I'm David West, new in town working with Susan Kramer at her detective agency. My job is to find out who murdered her father.'

The newsman nodded and shook West's hand. 'I'm Ira Haines. I knew Charlie, good man. Unfortunately nobody could find any clues as to who shot him.'

'Or maybe they didn't want to find them. There always are some kind of clues.' West went on trying to soften his words. 'What I need to do is go over your issues for two months before

Charlie's death. I'm looking for anything that might have been happening in town or the surrounding area that could have been big enough to set up a scandal or trigger some actions that were highly illegal. Something big enough for Charlie to get killed over.'

The newsman nodded, rubbed his nose, and made the ink smear larger. 'Yep, I tried the same thing. Went back over the time and the paper, and what I remembered. Came up with nothing.'

'There has to be something.'

'Make yourself at home. The files are right over there. This is Tuesday. I have to finish setting the front page by tonight or I'm in big trouble. I'll be out back if you want me.'

The redhead waved an ink stained hand and went through the door into the back shop.

West went to the files of papers. Each month was clipped between two dowels by date so they read first week to last. He went back five months and spread out the papers and began to read. He concentrated on the front pages only. Most of the papers were only eight pages. Now and then there would be a ten pager and sometimes one with only six.

He found city council meeting news, a new library, several train stories, and several items about a new spa that might open at a hot water springs just outside of town. The idea fell through the next month.

It took West an hour to check on those front pages. He found nothing that would have any huge economic value to anyone. Not a single story about something that would cause a scandal or ruin anyone's reputation.

The biggest story was about the railroad agreeing to put in a spur line a mile and a half to a new silver mine that had been proved out six months before. The spur line would shut down the mule pulled wagons that had been bringing out the ore to the siding near town.

There were several other mining

stories. He had heard about the Cripple Creek gold mines to the west and down near Colorado Springs. There seemed to be a lot of silver mining around as well. He knew little of mining and the stories didn't seem to have any bearing on the small town.

He put the papers away, thanked Ira the editor, and headed for the sheriff's office.

Sheriff Ramsden shook his head. 'We don't keep that kind of record here. Not a chance we could keep track when every man we send to the state penitentiary gets let out and where he goes. Not our affair.'

David West tried another tack. 'Do you know of any men who Charlie sent to prison who have served their time and come back to town to live?'

'Well now, I can come up with a few of those. Seems like a weak trail for you to follow. Yeah, thinking on it I can name four right off. I even have an idea where you might find them. Don't think it'll do you any good, though.'

'I have to check out every angle that I can find,' West said.

'Angus MacCloud is one. He served five years for beating to a bloody mess the young man who murdered his daughter. Most of the folks in town thought he should get a medal, but there was a strong anti-vigilante movement right then, so he got five years. He runs the hardware store here in town and is back at work.

'Another one is Rolfe Osgood. He went to the state pen for a year for stealing five hundred dollars from the little church he ran. He's back in the area. Owns a small ranch north of town. His wife and two sons kept it going while he was gone. Not much of a dangerous character, would you say?'

'I haven't met him. Sometimes the quiet ones can really hate.'

The sheriff stared at West. 'You sure don't know Reverend Osgood. He still runs his small no-denomination church.'

'Anybody else?'

'Yeah. Phil Eberhard. Phil deals cards at one of the saloons. Forget which one he's working right now. Phil went up for five years for second-degree murder. Shot up a saloon in a drunken brawl and killed the barkeep. Came back from prison snake mean. Gets in trouble regular, but so far he ain't killed nobody else.'

'Sounds like a gent I should meet,' West said.

The sheriff sent a brown stream of tobacco juice at a brass spittoon beside his desk. About half of it went in the target.

'Wouldn't go see him without a sidearm. Most men in your profession carry one.'

'I have one in my room.'

The sheriff shrugged. 'It's your hide.'

'You said four ex-convicts were back in town.'

'Yep, but I got to do me some figuring on the other one.'

West stood, thanked the lawman, and walked out to the street. He went directly to his hotel, took the six-gun from the attack the night before and found a small leather and gun shop down a half block.

The man moved from a shoe last and left a pair of women's high button shoes he had been repairing.

'Morning.'

'Yes, I have a weapon I want you to check out for me. Is it any good? Can I rely on it?'

West put the six-gun on the counter on fancy tooled leather.

'I'm Ned Burnett. You're new in town.' Burnett was in his thirties, had a black leather patch over one eye and a nasty livid scar across the opposite cheek. His one eye appraised West.

West pushed out his hand and shook. 'David West. I'm working with Susan Kramer.'

'Trying to find the killer, I'd wager. Good idea for you to have a fine six-gun.' Ned picked up the weapon and frowned, turned it over and stared hard at West.

'This your .45 revolver?'

'It is now. I found it last night.'

'Not likely. That's a known weapon, West. See those three notches cut into the wooden handle?'

'Yes.'

'Notches count for men this gun has killed. I've repaired this weapon for a gent here in town twice now. This man would not give up his Colt without a good fight.'

'Somebody tried to rob me last night in the dark. I objected and sent him running down the street. He may have a broken wrist.'

'Well now, so it was you.' Burnett chuckled. 'The man you took that gun away from calls himself Hondo. He's got a reputation around here. He's a kind of an enforcer. Somebody needs a bill collected, they give it to Hondo. He gets the money one way or another. Word is that he keeps half of what he collects. Been said that Hondo will do almost any job for money, including some rustling, some mine salting, even ‘dispose’ of a man somebody wants killed. Saw Hondo this morning with a cast on his right arm.’

West grinned. ‘Glad to hear it. He won’t be doing any fast draws for a while. I’ll give him back his gun, if he wants it. Might be interesting.’

‘Give it back?’

‘Yes, then I’ll know for sure he was the one who tried to hold me up. Now I better see about buying a shooter for myself. You have anything for sale?’

West came out of the store a half hour later with a six-gun on his hip in a well-used holster and gunbelt. It felt a little odd the way Burnett had told him to wear it, slung low on his right hip that way. The Colt .45 double action handled well. He’d have to get out of town and do some target practice. The weapon on his hip still felt strange to him, but at least it was low enough so it could be drawn easily.

Burnett said that Hondo usually spent most of his day at his ‘office’ in the Golden Dragon Saloon, a table well toward the back. West had taken the rounds out of Hondo's iron and pushed it into his belt on the left side. Now he walked a half block north and found the saloon open with a dozen clients already.

It was easy to spot the man with the starkly white hard plaster cast on his right arm. He sat at a back table talking with one of the waitresses. West walked directly to his table and the man started to get up when he saw West coming, but decided against it and slumped back in his chair. The woman scurried away.

Hondo looked smaller than West had figured. He was not over five six and slight, with a thin black moustache but otherwise clean shaven. Dark eyes stared at West as he stopped in front of the table. The man wore fancy cowboy duds, a gambler's red checked vest, and a low-crown, brown Stetson.

'Hear you lost your six-gun last night, Hondo,' West said, his tone even but tinged with steel.

'Might have. You find it?' Hondo's tone was neutral as he stared up at West.

'Actually I took it away from you when you tried to rob me out in front of the saloon. That's when I broke your wrist. I thought you had a reputation hereabouts.'

Hondo surged to his feet; his right arm, thick to the elbow with white plaster, held him back. He stopped the move and scowled. 'You'd be dead by now, you eastern dude, if I had a good right hand.'

'It was plenty good last night, and I'm still kicking. I'll sell your Colt to you for five hundred dollars.' West watched keenly as Hondo reacted. He started to rush forward then stopped and slammed his good fist on to the tabletop.

'West, you're a dead man, you just haven't stopped breathing yet.'

'Strong words from a crippled up has been.' West dropped Hondo's Colt on the table and snorted. 'Take this thing.

Obviously it's the only way you know how to do business. You try to use it on me again, and you'll be the one in a pine box.'

West turned his back on the seething man, waited a minute then turned back with a surly snarl. 'No hideout to shoot me in the back with your left hand? You're slipping, Hondo. Slipped for the last time, I'd say. Who's gonna hire you now except maybe some saloon as a swamper?'

West snorted and walked out of the saloon, the newly purchased Colt .45 slapping against his thigh.

Outside, he lifted his brows. So, he had a suspect who might have fired the shots. If Hondo did it, the murder was a job for hire, which didn't get him any closer to whoever might have hired him. But his little act would infuriate Hondo so much he might make a mistake and show the hand of whoever did hire him.

Now, West had three ex-convicts he should talk to. The sheriff didn't seem to think any would be productive. Who was the first one? He remembered the hardware store man, MacCloud, who went up for five years for attempted murder. Five years. A man could hold a mighty big grudge against the sheriff who sent him up.

Maybe he should stop by the office and let Susan know what he was doing. He walked that way. West was thinking about the case and not paying a lot of attention to others on the boardwalk, when suddenly something hard pressed against his chest. He stopped.

The street end of a man's cane prodded his chest, gently but in a commanding position. West looked up at once to see who held the cane. A booming voice froze him in place.

'Son, I think it's about time you and I had a long talk.'

4

The commanding voice of the man who held the cane against West's chest came from a gent not an inch over five feet. He wore a just pressed looking dark blue suit, white shirt, blue tie and had a white flower in his lapel. West figured he was over seventy years old.

'Son, you're working with Susie. I used to part time with Charlie Kramer and it's past due we have a set down and a good old fashioned talk out.'

The cane came down slowly and West saw that it was a practical, well-used walking stick, not one for show. The small man slumped slightly on his right foot and nodded.

'Yeah, I'm an old fart. I've learned a few things in my years and it's time you learned some of them too. Or you'll be six feet under our own boot hill before morning. I take it you want to be a detective, so there are a few basics you need to know now while you're still alive.'

West's face broke into a smile. 'My name's David West. Who may I ask are you?'

'Rocky, been known as Rocky for twenty years. Reckon it should work well enough for a few more. Let's step into the Kramer Agency over there and have our talk. Understand you not only broke Hondo's wrist, you took his gun away from him and insulted him a dozen times in public. That was not a smart thing to do. You ready to talk a little and listen a lot?'

Five minutes later, West learned that Rocky was one of Susan Kramer's long time friends. He had been a Pinkerton detective for ten years, then retired from the Denver office, and took a job with Sheriff Kramer there in Junction Springs as a deputy to taper off his working life.

'Son, figured there are some basics you got to know to stay alive. From there on it's just how smart you are and how fast you can learn how good a detective you'll be.'

Susan had been there when they walked in. She gave Rocky a big hug and a kiss on the cheek, then went and started the coffee. She stayed in the background and didn't say a word.

'So, you know the basic facts, West. Charlie was shot in the back of the head twice at close range. The killer must be someone the victim knew and trusted. No witnesses, evidently no evidence. At least none left now at this late date. You went to the first two good sources, the newspaper, and the new sheriff, where you probably got a bushel full of nothing.

'Now some basics in this detective work. You trust nobody. You believe nothing until it's proved. You take no favors from no one. You trust your own instincts. You learn how to use that new hogleg on your hip. We'll go out this afternoon and I'll teach you how to shoot it straight and fast. A fast draw ain't all that important. A straight shot hitting what you want to the first time is important. The three most important things you do as a detective are these: Number one: dig out the facts. Number two: dig out the facts. Number three: dig out the facts.'

Rocky stopped and looked up at West with a twinkle in his eyes.

'Son, you ain't said more than half a dozen words yet.'

'No time to get them into your interesting monologue.' They both laughed. Rocky pointed a lean, crooked finger at West. 'Why didn't I try to find the killer of my longtime friend? I'll tell you. Because I'm seventy-four, my heart ain't as good as it once was and I've got rheumatiz from sleeping on the hard, cold ground too often so I don't half well get around.'

Susan brought in the boiled coffee and Rocky sipped it. She rubbed his shoulders. He turned and nodded his thanks.

'Motive, West. You find a motive for

the killing and you'll find the murderer. That's what's had me stumped. Charlie wasn't working on any important case at the time. He didn't tell me about any big scandal building or a huge money deal anywhere. Any of them could be a motive. Dig up the motive and you'll get your killer.'

'I've been looking. Nothing in the paper.'

'Or nothing that was printed in the paper. Could be a difference. Maybe Ira Haines didn't know about a story, or maybe he didn't have all the facts yet so couldn't print it.

'Don't be misled by a clown like Hondo. Fact is Charlie would never have let Hondo get anywhere near him with a drawn gun, let alone behind his back. Hondo might have a hand in it, but he won't be the killer or the man behind the killer.'

'So where does that leave me?' West asked.

'With a shovel in your hands so you can start digging. Who were Charlie's best friends? Did he have a lady friend? Where did he invest any cash he might have had? Double-check his cases again for that month. Maybe he turned down a juicy one. Dig, dig, dig.'

Susan came up quickly with a file folder. 'Here are Dad's cases for the two months prior to his death. Not one of them the least bit major or suspicious. I've been over them a dozen times. Take a look.'

West began going through the typed and handwritten sheets. He studied each one, looked over at Rocky who would nod and they went on to the next one. About half way through, Rocky put his crooked finger on a typewritten page.

'The Warren-Hall Land Company,' Rocky said. 'What in tarnation is that?'

Susan frowned as she read the top of the sheet. 'Yes, I remember. Dad said it was the easiest hundred dollars he ever earned. All he had to do was confirm some iron corner stakes set in concrete, marking the boundaries of a piece of property. He hired a surveyor to check it out, confirmed the stakes within a half-inch of true, and signed the warrant. The land company paid the surveyor and then paid Dad. That was the end of it.'

'Never heard of this Warren-Hall Land Company,' Rocky said.

'We hadn't either. Dad said it was some Denver outfit new in the county and they wanted to be sure of their legal status on the property.'

'How much land and where is it?' West asked.

They all looked at the typed up report again.

'Uh huh,' Rocky said. 'I don't remember my legal descriptions too well, but it says it's a little over a mile square. That's six hundred and forty acres. A lot of land.'

'Any idea what they wanted to do with the land?' West asked.

Susan shook her head and sipped at her coffee. 'Dad said no big job. He did it in a day and was through with it.

That's why I could write up the report.'

'So what else?' Rocky asked.

They moved on. There was only one criminal case. Rocky remembered it. 'One of the lawyers in town asked Charlie to follow a man in a case of forgery. Charlie followed him for two days and made out his report. The man had been tried, convicted, and sent to prison for two years.'

The rest of the cases were simple information finding. One for a man who wanted his wife followed. One wife wanted the same thing for her husband. Both cases were finished and paid for and no follow up.

The three sat and nibbled at cookies Susan brought out and worked on a second cup of coffee. West began talking about land, property, deeds, and how they were recorded.

'Like most places, all land transactions must be recorded with the local county recorders office,' Rocky said. 'How can that help?'

West shrugged. 'Just thought if I

could find a pattern of someone buying up a lot of land in a special area . . . ' He shrugged again. 'Not much of an idea, huh?'

'Not bad, but it would take a couple of thousand hours of going over all the land records down there at the courthouse to dig out something like that.'

'Dig, dig, dig,' West said and grinned.

They all chuckled. The old man took a gold-filled railroad watch from his vest pocket, opened the case, and looked at it.

'We're wasting time. Let's go out back and do some target practice. You have some rounds for that .45?'

Twenty minutes later they were three long blocks from the last house of Junction Springs and facing a hillside smothered with aspen and pine.

'You ever shot a weapon before?' Rocky asked.

'Mostly shotguns and some deer hunting in Massachusetts,' West said. Rocky nodded.

'Good. Now, a handgun's got to be part of your arm. Got to grow right out of your fingers and palm. You got to know where it is and how to get to it. When you scratch your elbow or your nose you don't have to fumble around to find them. You just know. Same way should be when your hand goes for your Colt. Don't have to be no lightning draw. We ain't got nobody who can fast draw in town. Hondo is the best and he's a slacker compared to a real gunman.

'But you got to know where your side arm is, how to get it out of the holster as fast as possible, aim, and shoot. Let's see you draw that weapon. First let me take the rounds out of it.'

After the weapon was unloaded and back in leather, West tried. He looked down at the Colt and Rocky shook his head.

'Not a chance, West. You can't look at your gun. You're supposed to be watching the man who is about to kill you. Don't look down. Know where it is. Try it again. See that skinny pine over there? He's your gunman. Watch him and then draw.'

West tried it and the Colt tumbled to the ground. He went through it again, glancing down as he drew, getting the butt of the weapon in his palm, pulling the Colt out just enough so the barrel cleared the leather. His hand gripped the handle and his finger pushed into the trigger guard. Then he pushed it forward to aim at the tree.

'Again, again and again until I think you can do it without shooting off your foot, lad. I'd say about twenty times and you'll start getting it down.'

It took him twenty-five. By then the slap of the Colt's handle into his fingers and palm felt almost natural. He did it again and Rocky nodded.

'Now, lad, this is a double action weapon. All you need to do is pull the trigger and that cocks the trigger and lets the hammer fall on the round. But the best way is to cock the Colt as you bring it up to fire. Saves time when you pull the trigger. Half a second? Could be the difference between living and dying. As you feel the barrel riding up the leather, reach with your thumb for the burred end of the hammer, and draw it back until it clicks. That's all there is to it. Give it a try, but keep that thing aimed downrange.'

This time it went faster. After ten tries, he had the weapon cocked by the time he pulled it out of leather, and started to aim.

Rocky nodded. 'You're a good man with guns, West. That Navy training you told me about is still with you. Now, let's get to aiming. You don't have a lot of time. No lifting the weapon shoulder high and sighting through the notch. No time. Use the point and shoot method.'

'What?'

'As you lift the six-gun, point your hand at the target. Simple as that. Like you're pointing your finger at something. It's all eye and hand coordination and you'll be surprised how well it works.'

He tried it and grinned. After three point and aim tries, Rocky had West put five rounds back in the weapon.

'Try it. I'll give you a go, and you draw and shoot that killer tree out there.'

West nodded as a sudden line of sweat popped out on his head. Did he have to do this? Was he going to get in a gunfight and maybe get shot? He took a deep breath. At least he should know how to use the weapon.

He stood loose the way Rocky had taught him, feet eighteen inches apart, knees slightly bent.

The 'go' came before he was ready. He pulled up on the Colt as he'd done before, felt it clear leather and cocked the hammer with his thumb, then all in the same motion point-aimed at the tree and squeezed the trigger. The weapon went off and kicked high in the air.

'Wow,' West said. 'It's got a real kick.'

'Hold it tight so it doesn't rise on you that much. See where your round went? It was three feet to the right of the tree. You pulled the trigger instead of squeezing it and pulled the barrel a fraction of an inch to the right. At that distance that means three or four feet. Try it again.'

For more than an hour West drew, aimed, and fired. Drew, aimed, and fired. He reloaded six rounds in the chambers now, then drew, aimed, and fired again.

It took him twenty rounds before he hit the tree the first time. He stood roughly 30 feet away. Now Rocky moved him up ten feet.

'Most six-guns are best at not more than twenty feet. With the short barrel, the smallest miss-aim throws the round off a foot or two feet. Never get into a serious gunfight at more than twenty feet. If you have protection, then crank away at forty feet, but don't expect many hits. You've done enough for today.'

'Good, a couple of gents I need to talk to.'

'Who,' Rocky asked.

'Three men who were sent to prison by Charlie and are back in town now.'

'Yeah, Rolfe Osgood would be one. Not much of a threat there. Actually most people think Rolfe is a bit short of a full bushel when it comes to brain power.'

They walked back into the rear door of the detective agency and found Susan at her desk having a quiet talk with a young woman.

West waved at her and started out the front door, then thought of something, took out his six-gun, and removed the sixth round from the last chamber. He'd never forget again about carrying his weapon with the hammer on the empty cylinder.

Rocky waved at him and took his coffee cup to the back room for a refill.

West went to the hardware store half a block down and across the street. In the early West, hardware stores had sprung up to fill in the chinks for building and repair needs that most of the early general stores couldn't stock. Now they had established themselves as the place for tools and hinges and nails and screws and all sorts of things that a homeowner or a builder of stores and houses might need.

Inside the establishment, West found himself admiring a set of six-inch butt hinges for a door. They were solid brass and sturdy enough to hold an oak panel. Someone hurried up near him and cleared his throat.

'Needing something today, sir?' the man asked.

'Not really,' West said. 'Actually I'm looking for Angus MacCloud. Is that you?'

'Indeed it is. Owner of this store and property. What might I do for you this afternoon?' MacCloud wore a white shirt and tie. Garters held his shirt cuffs away from his hands. He had on a green eyeshade over a thick mantle of dark hair. He wore long sideburns, but otherwise was clean-shaven. His eyes showed brown and he was in his late forties. MacCloud stood about five eight on the slender side.

West held out his hand. 'My name is David West and I work for the Kramer Detective Agency. I'm investigating the murder of Charlie Kramer.'

'Good. I had some differences with the sheriff, but that's all over and done with. Charlie was a good man, once a good friend. Hate to see him killed that way. Somebody should pay. I'll be glad to do whatever I can to help you.'

'Good. Do you know of anyone who hated Charlie so much he would shoot the man in the back?'

'Nope. Thought about it a good deal. Figure I'd be a suspect, but the new sheriff never even talked to me. Must be something brewing in town we don't know about. Maybe Charlie got a line on it and they killed him to shut him up.'

'Good idea, but who did it and what's the important element that caused all the trouble?'

'Not an idea in the world. Thought some on that problem as well. I come up with a blank page.'

West listened carefully to the man's words, his tone, and his manner. MacCloud seemed to have nothing to hide. He spoke the truth. The fledgling detective thanked him.

'If you think of anything that might give me a lead, be sure to drop by at the Kramer office and tell me.'

The merchant said he would.

West made a detour to the Thompson General Store and bought a new pair of cowboy boots; they had his size and seemed to fit. The clerk said if they pinched too much he could bring them back the next day and get the next bigger size.

He bought two pair of jeans and two more shirts so he could blend in with this Western town and hurried back to the office. Susan was there and worried.

'You saw that woman who was here when you passed through? She's Hattie

Younger, Mrs Ellis Younger, wife of the mayor's son. The mayor, Pelton Younger is our town's richest man. Owns several businesses and runs the local politics.'

'So why was the younger Mrs Younger here to see you?'

'She says her husband hasn't touched her in a month. Says she's sure he has a floozy somewhere here in town. She wants us to follow him and find the Jezebel.'

'Just the job for you, Susan.'

'I can't. Ellis Younger knows me. I went to school with him and Hattie. You have to do it.'

'I'm trying to find your father's killer.'

'I know. This won't take more than a day or two.'

Somebody pushed open the agency door and burst in. The man was grinning, hair wild, no hat and he looked around until he saw West.

'Hey, you David West? You best get your britches outside. Hondo is out there telling everyone that you're a yellow belly and he's calling you out for a showdown. Right here and right now.'

West touched the Colt on his hip and snorted. 'That's not possible. I broke Hondo's wrist last night. Not a chance he can fire a six-gun.'

'Then come on out and tell him yourself,' the messenger screeched. He let out a warhoop and hurried back outside.

West shrugged. 'Can't be,' he said. 'I best check it out and see what's going on.'

5

David West hesitated before he went through the front door. He looked at Susan who stood by her desk, a frown etching her pretty face.

'Don't go out there. Hondo's a killer.' Her frown deepened, lines showed on her forehead and her eyes blinked as if holding back tears.

'Not much way I can stay in here now,' West said. 'Don't worry, he can't shoot with a broken wrist.'

West pushed through the door and felt the warm sun on his face. The area had suddenly filled with men and a few women. Twenty of them stood on the boardwalk on each side of the street waiting for the showdown to start. Hondo stood in the middle of the dusty avenue, feet apart, arms at his sides. His white cast showing plainly on his right forearm and covering most of his hand.

His left arm hung loosely near his left hip and a holstered six-gun that rested there. Hondo could shoot left-handed?

'There comes the coward now,' Hondo shouted. 'Told you he was yellow-bellied, but he's still man enough to come when he's called out.'

West paused on the boardwalk. Hondo stood glowering fifty feet down the street. West took a deep breath and stepped off the boards into the dust and walked toward Hondo. He was thirty feet away from the gunman when somebody shouted from the crowd.

'Sure looks like Kid Stingaree to me,' the voice called. Hondo turned toward the sound, shrugged, and then stared at West again.

Another voice came out that sounded like Rocky.

'I seen him shoot once in Cripple Creek. Blasted away so fast I hardly saw him draw. Then the other gent was on the ground dead as a turkey buzzard at breakfast.'

Hondo turned toward the voices.

'What you guys blathering about?' He called.

'Nothing about you Hondo,' the voice came back. 'Just talking about Kid Stingaree, fastest gunslinger I ever seen. This gent is a dead ringer for him. Course you know he changes his name and his looks now and then. Hard to tell what he's called now or for sure what he looks like.'

Hondo frowned, turned, and stared at West. 'You, yeah you who says you're David West. You ever go by another name?'

West settled in twenty feet from Hondo, his legs spread, knees slightly bent and his right hand hovering over the gun-metal on his right hip.

'Been known to use other names. What's it to you, dead man?'

'Saw him once outside of Denver take on two shooters at once,' the voice that sounded like Rocky came out of the crowd again. 'Nailed one of them with his first shot, dove and rolled and made the other *hombre* miss. Then he gut shot the second one and laughed while the guy took an hour to die.'

Hondo looked at West, then back at the crowd.

'Ask him if he's ever used the Kid Stingaree name,' somebody called.

Hondo began to sweat. He lifted his black Stetson and resettled it, then looked at West again. He moved his left hand away from his six-gun.

'Yeah, West. You ever use the name of Kid Stingaree?'

'You didn't call him out, you called out David West. Let's get on with this. I've got things to do.'

Hondo moved his left hand higher, held onto his white cast. 'Well now. Seems there might have been a misunderstanding here. You going by the name of West? How was I to know you might be somebody else? Don't mean to cause all that much of a fuss.' West stood there, his hand still near his six-gun.

'You called me out, Hondo. You going to stand there and shoot, or you going to crawl away with your tail between your legs?'

'Right handed I'd go up against you, Kid. Not with my left. Out of practice with my left.'

'You putting an end to your challenge and apologizing for calling me a yellow-bellied coward?'

'Yes. Yes. How was I supposed to know who you really are? OK, you ain't no coward. I take it back. That good enough?'

'No. Take that iron out careful with thumb and finger and drop it in the dust. Then get off the street.'

'Drop my gun . . . ?' Hondo shrugged, lifted the Colt from leather and dropped it on the ground. He turned and marched quickly back to the boardwalk and into the Laughing Lady Saloon.

The crowd mumbled. West stood there a moment more, then turned and walked back to the Kramer Detective Agency and went inside.

Susan ran to him and threw her arms around him. 'I never thought I'd see you alive again,' she said. She hugged him tightly then stepped back, color rising out of her neck into her face.

'Oh, sorry.'

West grinned. 'I'm not sorry. Best hug I've had in weeks. Now who is Kid Stingaree?'

The front door opened and Rocky limped in. His grin was splattered all over his face.

'You've never heard of Kid Stingaree?' Rocky asked. He slid into a chair, gave a big sigh, and tapped his cane on the edge of a desk. 'The Kid is a shootist of the old school. Plenty good with his six-gun, works for either side of the law, has the best reputation of any gunner out there right now. He's been in Denver and 'round about these parts for three or four years. Most folks know about him but not many can say they know for sure who he is.'

'So that was you in the crowd talking about the Kid?' West asked.

Rocky chuckled. 'I couldn't let Hondo blow your head off, now, could

I? Figured I better do something. Hondo is no slouch with his left hand firing a six-gun. Not as fast as with his right but still faster than most men. I forgot to tell you that.'

'Thanks.'

'None needed. You can't help us find Charlie's killer being in an extreme case of dead and buried. So, how's our case coming along?'

'Not well. So far I'm finding a lot of people who didn't do it.'

'Motive, find the motive,' Rocky said.

'I've still got a problem here, if you two will listen to me,' Susan said, one fist propped on her hip, her face worried.

'That would be the younger Mrs Younger,' West said. 'You said her husband knows you. How about Rocky for that assignment? He's hanging around, might as well put him to use.'

'I'm retired,' Rocky said and pinched his eyes partly shut. 'Who did you say? Hattie Younger? Now there is a pretty woman.'

'So follow her husband for a few days

and help her out,' Susan said.

Rocky nodded. 'Might just do that. Hear he spends some time at cards over at the Golden Dragon. Do I get any expense money for playing poker?'

Susan shook her head. Rocky shrugged. 'Didn't think so. Maybe I should mosey over there and see if he's playing. He messing around with some woman, right?'

Susan nodded. 'We need her name and address. Shouldn't be too hard for an experienced Pinkerton detective like you.' She said it with a grin and Rocky waved at them and limped out the front door.

After Rocky left, West went to the county courthouse and talked with the county recorder. The man carried a sharpened pencil behind his right ear. West wondered how it stayed there.

'No sir, not that I remember. I'd recall if there were a lot of transactions on any one parcel or section of the county. I work with these big record books all day.'

'Now, educate me here,' West said. 'A deed must be recorded here when it changes hands, by sale, gift or inheritance. Is that right?'

'Absolutely. We know who owns every square foot of this county.'

'What about homesteads?'

'Got to be registered here, too. Not much of that going on anymore.'

'What about leases, rentals, mining claims, oil rights?'

'We don't deal with leases or rentals. But if somebody puts down stakes for a mining claim, it's got to be recorded here. Never had any oil rights, but my guess is they would have to be recorded, too.'

'Fine. I may check again with you about any large-scale property sales in one area. Part of a study that I'm doing on land values.' He said goodbye and went out into the sunshine.

What next? Dig, dig, dig. Only he had to have something to dig for or some place to dig. He went to the back of the courthouse to the sheriff's office.

The county's top lawman was there.

'I thought of that fourth man who had been sent to prison by Charlie Kramer and came back to town,' Sheriff Ramsden said. 'Guy by the name of Fred Ihander. He runs the livery stables at the north edge of town. Angry little man. Be careful what you say to him. He's touchy about being in prison.'

'Good, I'll give him a call.' West looked away not quite sure how to ask the next question. He lifted his brows and watched the lawman. 'Sheriff, you've been around town a while. You know of anything strange going on? Like anything that somebody could make a lot of money from?'

'Don't know what you mean, West.'

'Not sure myself. I'm looking for anything that might have some bearing on why Charlie Kramer was murdered. Flailing away at the whole stack of hay trying to find a needle.'

'You picked a good one for your first job in town. Hear that I missed quite a show in the street this morning. That all true about Hondo trying to call you out, then backing down?'

'Some say, Sheriff.'

The lawman grinned. 'Even I've heard of Kid Stingaree. Somehow you don't look quite right for the part. But then again . . . Way I hear it is that this Kid Stingaree uses a lot of disguises and changes his hair cut and even hair color. That way the lawmen and the outlaws are never sure who he is.'

'I've been hearing the same thing.'

'But you don't deny that you're Kid Stingaree.'

West laughed and stood. 'Don't rightly deny it, don't rightly agree to it. What other folks think about me is mostly their business. I try never to pry.'

West walked to the door and touched the brim of his low crowned Stetson. 'Been good talking with you, Sheriff. Might just go out and see this Fred Ihander.'

The Junction Spring livery was not in

good repair. As he walked up to it, West noted the boards loose on the barn, the fences that needed work, a corral that had lost its top rail half way around. There were three dusty buggies with weeds growing around them sitting beside the barn in the open waiting to be hired. The first pasture behind the barn had a sprinkling of horses, none that looked too sturdy to West's way of thinking.

He had done a lot of riding, but mostly on carefully groomed and proper thoroughbreds. The quarter horse would be something new to him.

He walked into the open barn door and saw a small office to the left. A man sat behind a cluttered desk waving a small fan at himself. His feet were propped on the desk and he had a bottle of beer in one hand. He looked up and nodded.

'You sure don't look like Kid Stingaree to me. No offense, just an observation. What can I do for you?'

'Fred Ihander?'

The man sipped the beer, and only then nodded.

'Understand you did some mining hereabouts.'

The feet dropped off the desk and banged on the floor. He came to his feet. A scowl started on his face then faded. Ihander dropped the fan and sipped at the beer.

'Some.'

'Enough to own a mine or two and get in a spot of trouble?'

'True. Done and over. Did my time on that one. I was just trying to recover what the guy I bought it for suckered me out of. So what?'

'You come back to town mad at Sheriff Kramer?'

Ihander laughed, tipped the beer bottle, drained it, and threw it out the door.

'Mad? No. I took a chance, he caught me. No, I didn't gun down Kramer. He even rented a buggy from me now and then. Had a lady he squired around a mite.'

'Any gold left in these hills?'

'Gold is where you find it. Crazy Bob Womack proved that to a lot of folks over in Cripple Creek. Figure there's more to be found, if'n a body knows where to look. Me, I'm getting too old and cantankerous to even go looking.'

'Did Kramer know much about mining?'

'Enough to nail me to the wall. Seems he knew more about gold mining than he let on. Got me convicted, that's for sure.'

'Any idea who shot Kramer?'

'A sheriff makes enemies, lots of them. Not all of them wind up in prison.'

'Somebody right here in town?'

'Could be. Now I figure whoever shot Kramer knew him well enough to walk behind his back. Kramer wasn't stupid. If he was on to something that would make a man rich, he wouldn't hesitate to protect himself.'

'So it could have been Kramer's good friend?'

'Or a new business partner.'

'Curious. I hadn't thought of that.'

They stood there a minute looking at each other. West nodded. 'Yeah, I believe you. Now, I'll be needing a horse tomorrow to ride out to see Rolfe Osgood at his ranch. This where I come to rent one?'

'This is the place.' Ihander reached in a drawer of the desk and took out a bottle of beer and tossed it to West. It was a local product and had the spring-loaded ceramic and rubber cap that sprung back on wires. Ihander took out another one and opened it for himself.

'Sit and rest yourself.'

West sat down on a chair and opened the beer. Not bad for being so warm. He took a draw then looked at Ihander.

'Hear you don't know beans yet about who killed Kramer, that right?' Ihander asked.

'Real close. I was hoping you shot him.'

They both laughed.

'You figure it was a for hire job?' Ihander asked.

'Nope. Not with that back shooting and friendship idea. Whoever did it had to be a big player in whatever game it was. I figure Kramer tumbled to some scheme, something illegal or close to it, and before he could expose it, or maybe try to worm his way in as a partner, they killed him.'

'What's that valuable around here?' Ihander asked. He frowned. 'If it ain't silver or gold, how about timber? Some good stands of timber on some federal and state lands.'

'In the county?' West asked.

'Yeah.'

'But for mineral or timber rights, you'd have to control the property. County recorder said there hasn't been any large scale land buys in any area of the county.'

'That puts the kybosh on that then. What else is there?'

'Some other minerals?' West asked. 'Lead, zinc, copper?'

'Never been any of those around here. Wrong type of mountains, they tell me.'

West finished the warm beer and stood. Ihander stayed in his chair and put his feet up on the desk. He squinted up at West.

'You never told me if you're Kid Stingaree or not. Never known him to be working as a detective.'

West took off his hat and wiped a bead of perspiration away and settled the topper at just the right angle.

'You ever known him not to be a detective?' West waved and walked out the door without an answer. So most people in town would wonder about him now. It could give him an edge. Nobody would push him too hard wondering if he was the famed gunman.

He grinned and touched the .45 Colt in his holster. The bluff about being Kid Stingaree would work just as long as he didn't have to get in a shoot-out with somebody.

Walking back to town, he realized that he'd missed lunch again. He stopped at the first cafe he saw, had a big roast beef sandwich and two cups of coffee, and made it back to the Kramer Detective Agency office just before two o'clock.

Susan looked up when he came in. 'You've been busy. The desk clerk from the hotel stopped by with an envelope for you. Said it had been in your box since this morning and figured it might be important.'

'Oh? Who would write me a note?'

She handed him the plain white envelope and he tore it open.

He unfolded a piece of paper that could have come from a schoolboy's tablet and read the block lettering in pencil.

'Mr West. If you want to know more about Charlie Kramer's death, go to a small canyon in back of the deserted mine called Hannah's Hades. Be there at five o'clock today.'

There were directions how to find it

about four miles north of town just off the old stage road to Denver. He showed the note to Susan.

'You're not going. It sounds like a trap.'

'I'm at a dead end here. If it is a trap, I'll have to capture whoever is out there and make him talk. It's the best lead I've had so far.'

'It says four miles out. Take you an hour to ride out there.'

'I better get started.'

'Take a rifle. Get one at Pallow's and some rounds for it.'

'I have a rifle and I'll get a horse from Fred Ihander out at the livery. I just met him.' West watched Susan. 'This is what I have to do. Best chance we have to get something really solid. I can take care of myself. I was in the navy for two years, did I tell you that? Now don't worry.'

He turned to go, saw Susan blinking and he hurried out the front door and ran to the hotel to get his rifle and rounds. Yes, he had to do this, so he could get it over with and get back to Boston. Many times in the past week he had been able to think of little else but Jane Poindexter and wondering who had killed her. Who had stolen the life right out of him? Who had killed his love and wife to be? He'd find out. He had to. But first, he had to discover who killed Charlie Kramer.

6

25 June, 1895

He had ridden the four miles out to Hannah's Hades and was about to dismount at the old well they told him to stop at when a rifle shot cracked into the still air. The round missed as it whispered past him. Before he could react a second slug hit his horse and the third blasted through the fleshy part of his upper left arm and jolted him out of the saddle.

He hit the ground hard holding onto the rifle and his six-gun, and then scrambled behind a big ponderosa log. He was safe for the moment. He tried to wait them out but he knew that wouldn't work. So he had to charge away from the log heading what he hoped was no more than fifty feet to the thick stand of pines and brush downslope from the shooters. He carried his pistol in one hand and the new Remington repeating rifle in the other as he charged forward.

A rifle round hit a rock just ahead of him as he zig-zagged toward the safe haven. The lead slug whined away into the hill. Two more shots sliced through the air past him and another tore at his shirt sleeve but missed flesh.

He thought he would never get to the trees. He waited for that one round to jolt into his back, snap his spine and sprawl him lifeless in the rocks and grass on this Colorado wilderness.

Eight or nine more shots slanted at him but all missed and he plunged into the trees and dove to the ground for more protection.

Now things could even out a little. He brought up the rifle and hefted it. He'd used a better one hunting, but this would do. He squirmed around a foot-thick ponderosa and looked up the hill and across the small gully. He spotted a puff of gunpowder smoke and heard the report of a rifle. The round went wide and high. He sighted in on the spot with the Remington where he had seen the shooter and waited. A moment later a figure lifted up with a rifle to fire again. West had to adjust his sight only an inch to the left and squeeze the trigger. The figure jolted backward and out of sight. West didn't know if he hit the bushwhacker or only scared him.

He rolled to the side to a new spot and pushed some brush aside so he could see past a tree trunk. Twenty feet down from where the first man had fired he saw movement, then a quick lift up by a man and a rifle fired. The round went well uphill from him.

He waited again and when the man lifted up to fire again, he jolted a round at him. This time he heard a scream and the man rose up then fell forward over a log he had been behind. He didn't move.

For one resounding moment, he realized that he had just killed a man. It hit him like a jolt of lightning, stunning him for a few seconds. Then the other man fired four times as fast as he could work his weapon and the rounds zapped through the trees and branches West hid under. It brought him out of his daze. He'd deal with the death later. Right now it was his own life he was more worried about.

Could he get behind the last man? Was the one on the near cliff wounded or dead? He studied the area. The small ravine grew larger as it went downhill. At one place twenty yards down the quaking aspen and the ponderosa pine grew in a swath across the gully. A perfect cover for him to cross over and move up the hill on the other side with the hopes of getting behind the shooters.

He moved quickly but without making any of the brush jiggle or sway. When he came to the screen of brush and trees it was not as thick as he had hoped. He ran from one grown ponderosa to the next, pausing a moment, then surging out again. There was no fire, no indication he had been seen.

The man on the hill fired again into the area where West had vanished. The stock broker-turned-detective grinned. Fooled him.

It took him five more minutes to slip up the slope and move out of some brush and aspen so he could see the area where the bushwhackers had settled down. First he saw two horses well down from the gunmen. Then he saw the dead body draped over the log.

Up the hill ten yards a second man hunkered down behind another fallen ponderosa. It must have been four feet thick and towered a hundred feet in the air when alive. Now it offered three feet of shooter protection — from the front.

Should he call out to the man and warn him he was covered and he should throw down his weapon? West decided at once he would not do that. The bushwhackers hadn't given him any warning. His arm hurt like fire now that he wasn't rushing around. He lifted the rifle and sighted in on the man's back. The shooter below fired again at the brush where West had vanished. For a moment the bushwhacker looked at his partner, and then fired again.

West stroked the trigger on the Winchester and saw the big slug hit the gunman in the right shoulder and spin him around, dump him to the ground, with his rifle still resting on the big log. The gunman started to crawl.

'Hold it right there,' West barked using his field command military voice. 'Don't move an inch or I'll drill another round right through your spine.'

The man stopped. West drew his Colt and stood, working his way carefully down the slope, watching the dead man, looking across the gully at the ridge, but nobody moved. West stared at the wounded man on the ground. He wore range-roughed pants, a blue shirt and a low crowned dirty cowboy hat. When he turned to look at West, he showed a full beard and mustache, a thin nose and shifting eyes.

'Who hired you to kill me?' West barked.

The man jumped and rolled over. He held both hands up. 'No hideout. I ain't got no other weapon.'

'Who hired you to kill me?' West punctuated the words with a .45 slug digging into the dirt a foot from the man's head.

'Oh, no. Don't kill me. Just a job. Nothing personal.'

'Terribly personal to me, you stinking bushwhacker. Tell me who hired you or you're dead and rotting right here.'

'No, don't shoot. Some guy in a saloon. Gave us fifty dollars each and all we had to do was gun you down.'

'What did the man look like?'

'Dunno. Dark in there. Maybe average height, clean shaven.'

'A cowboy or a towner?'

'Oh, man from town. Talked real swell like. Now get me to a doctor before I bleed to death.'

'Dead for you might be better than

fifteen years in the state prison. Was this guy old or young?'

'Maybe in his forties, wore a town suit and tie.'

'You see him around town?'

'No, I just got in yesterday myself.'

'Which saloon was it?'

'That I remember. The Laughing Lady Saloon.'

'OK, stand up and show me where your horses are.'

It took them ten minutes to get to the horses. West brought both the outlaws' rifles with him. He tied the reins of the one horse to the saddlehorn of the other. His own mount was dead, so he rode the dead outlaw's horse. He boosted the wounded man into the saddle and tied his hands to the pommel.

'Don't try to get away or I'll shoot you dead, you understand? You're tied to my mount so don't try anything.'

It was a slow ride into town. Now that the crisis was over, West realized his left arm was almost useless. It hurt like fire and he had done little to stop the flow of blood. For a moment he felt dizzy, but he jolted that away with a shake of his head. If he passed out now, he was dead. He tightened his legs on the horse and balanced the weapons across the saddle and rode on.

An hour later in town he stopped in front of the sheriff's office and told the gunman to stay right where he was. A curious man looked at the two wounds and whistled.

'Some gunplay here, I'd guess,' the man said. He was in his fifties, bald and wearing a white shirt and no hat.

'True. Would you get the sheriff or a deputy out here right away?'

The man bobbed his head. 'Glad to,' he said and ran into the court house.

A half hour later the man who gave his name as Shorty Colton was safely in a jail cell charged with attempted murder. He gave no more information about who had hired him. Doctor Eaton had been there and treated both gunshot wounds. He wrapped West's arm and nodded.

'Funny strange how a slug can go through an arm like that and just make little holes on both sides, never touch a vital nerve or artery and miss the bone completely. You should be in fighting trim in two weeks. No heavy lifting with that left arm. Shorty's arm is another case. Gonna hurt him a long time.'

Sheriff Ramsden stroked his beard after the doctor left. 'You say they left you a message and you walked right into three guns? Where are the other two gents?'

'One is dead for sure and the other one I think I hit. Didn't see any more of him. I'll go out and bring in the dead one. Might get some interesting townsfolk reaction.'

'Maybe tomorrow. Today you'll get caught in the dark. Tomorrow I'll have a deputy ride out with you with a spare horse to bring back one, maybe two bodies. Then you'll have to write out a report for me about what happened.'

'About eight o'clock?'

'Sounds good. You can turn in that horse you rode to the livery to replace your rented one that got killed. Fred will appreciate it. The other one is county property as long as this jasper is in jail. Tell Fred about it. We've done this before.'

After West put the horses away and stashed his rifle at the detective agency, he sauntered into the Laughing Lady and talked to the barkeep.

The man was heavy, sweating, with shirt sleeves rolled up, full jowls, and eyes squeezed half shut by the flesh. He wiped the bar and squinted at West.

'You a new guy in town,' he said. 'First beer is on the house. My place. Name is Willy Wilson.'

West held out his hand and took the oversized paw. 'West, David West. I'm working with Susan at the detective agency.'

'Yeah, I heard. Doing any good?'

'Almost got killed this afternoon.' He explained what happened. 'Shooter said he was hired in here last night by some clean-shaven town gent with fifty dollar bills in his pockets. You notice anybody like that here last night?'

'Hey, I sell beer, booze. The customer pays his money and I don't notice who does what. I live longer that way. Right?'

'Yeah, Willy, you will, I might not. Any gents, big town guys in here last night? Think back, anybody surprise you?'

'Yeah, a couple, but I don't tell tales. Sorry. Good luck. How's the beer?'

* * *

Kramer Detective Agency was closed when West went by before supper. He had a good meal and a long night's sleep in the hotel. The loaded six-gun was two inches from his hand all night.

The next morning he picked up Deputy Ken Lawton and they rode out to the old Hannah's Hades mine trailing a pack horse behind them. The bushwhacker was still draped over the log and stiff now from rigor mortis. They bent him over the saddle of the pack horse and tied him on.

'Where was the third bushwhacker?' Lawton asked.

It took them twenty minutes of scrambling up the side of the ravine to get to the ledge where the man had fired from. They found a lot of scuff marks in the dirt and rocks, the remains of what looked like part of a sandwich and an empty flip top beer bottle.

'Here and gone,' Lawton said.

'Thought I winged him. He jolted backwards.'

Lawton looked at a brown spot on the ground near the ledge.

'My bet is you drew some blood,' Lawton said. 'Look at this. Dried blood or my mother isn't a Presbyterian.'

'So he probably earned his fifty dollars and skedaddled on to the next town.'

'Figures.'

When they rode into the village an hour and a half later, they attracted a crowd that followed them to the court house. By the time they had unloaded the corpse and bent it straight and placed it on the boardwalk, there were twenty people staring at the man.

'Bushwhacker,' Deputy Lawton said which was explanation enough for everyone.

West held back away from the crowd and watched everyone who took a close look at the corpse. Some shook their heads, others laughed, and one woman almost fainted. The biggest reaction came from a man wearing a black suit, white shirt, blue tie, and an English bowler. He carried a walking stick and stared at the body for some time, then whirled and marched away straight to an office. His face was a contorted mask of fury when he passed West and he was mumbling to himself. He went into the office and slammed the door. West walked past the place. The sign on it proclaimed in gold lettering: 'Victor Charest, lawyer.'

When he walked into the Kramer Detective Agency office he found Susan and Rocky having coffee.

'Charest?' Rocky blurted out in reaction to West's question. 'He's the best lawyer in town, maybe in the whole state. And he's also the most under-handed, double dealing and crookedest one to boot. I wouldn't trust him with my piggy bank.'

'What about the derby wearer with the fancy walking stick?'

'D'know his name,' Rocky said. 'He's been in town a couple of months. English as they come. Didn't know he knew Charest.'

'Are we starting to smell big money here?' West asked.

'If it's crooked big cash, then Charest would be in on it,' Rocky said. 'How does the Englisher fit in?'

'Charest have lots of money?'

'Not lately. He's not hurting. But no big stack of greenbacks.'

'Maybe the English gent is the money tree.'

A boy about sixteen with a flopping shirt and no shoes hurried into the detective office.

'Is Mr West here?' he asked.

'Me.'

The boy handed him an envelope and turned and ran out the door leaving it open behind him.

West started after him, and then changed his mind when he saw the printed stationery of the Bruno County Recorder's office. He opened the envelope and read the note.

'County recorder says three pieces of land just changed hands. He wants to see me.'

'Big chunks of real estate?' Rocky asked.

'That's what I asked him to watch for. I better check this out. I'll be back.'

West adjusted the gunbelt on his hip, steadied the Colt in its leather holster and went out the door into the street.

* * *

'Yes, sir, Mr West. Three large parcels of land changed hands and I recorded them today. Papers came in by mail. All three are three hundred and twenty acres or more and adjacent to one another. That's over a square mile and a half.'

'Whereabouts are these parcels?'

'All are to the west and north of us, up in some rugged ridges and ravines not good for much. Sure not cattle country. The closest edge is about six miles north of here. The new owner is the Warren-Hall Land Company with a Denver address.'

'Any of the principals listed on the deed?'

'Nope. Have to go to the state to get those names of the officers of the corporation.'

West thanked the clerk and went back to the office.

'The new owners are the same ones who Charlie Kramer did that one day of work for and got the hundred dollars,' West told Susan. 'The Warren-Hall Land Company of Denver.'

'That makes it sound suspicious,' she said.

'I'm riding out there to see if there's any development going on, anybody camped out there, or any cattle involved.'

'Don't get lost up in there. A million little canyons and arroyos.'

'Want to be my guide?'

She laughed. 'Afraid not. Been a long time since I've ridden six miles, let along twelve. Have fun.'

* * *

An hour and a half later he realized it wasn't fun. The sun boiled down on him, a slight wind blew sand in his face, and he couldn't find any sign of habitation or development. So far it was just raw land, and not much to look at to boot. Steep canyons sparsely sprinkled with some ponderosa. Almost no flat land. One ridge after another ascending into a range of mountains that had snow on their south slopes. He took one more look from a ridge where he could see the other parcels to the north. Nothing there, not a thing.

He snorted, turned his mount around and rode back the way he had come. Riding to town seemed like twice as far as going out.

It was just before five o'clock when he had the horse stabled and walked in the detective office. Susan was there.

'Nothing,' she said. 'You must have found absolutely nothing but raw land from your expression.'

He slumped in a chair and nodded. 'Yeah, right. Not a thing but some trees, ridges, gullies and ravines. Why would anybody pay good money for those parcels?'

'So it's not timber, can't be for cattle. That only leaves mining.'

'My mining source says no silver or gold out there, and it's the wrong type of land for any other minerals. So what are they doing with a square mile and a half of ridges and gullies?'

'West, you need a break. Come to my place for supper. I've been cooking some baked beans all day over a slow fire. They should be done now. Wait until you try them. Some bacon in them, some brown sugar, chopped onions and a touch of barbeque sauce. You haven't lived until you bite down on these beans.'

'Any fresh bread and a pad of butter?'

'You got it, cowboy.' She nodded. 'Yep, you've changed. You even look more at home now in those jeans and shirt. The hat doesn't hurt. Now, let's close up here and go see if those beans are done. Some boiled potatoes and those new carrots I have should help. Did I tell you about the fresh cherry pie I just made?'

West grinned in spite of his sour mood. The case was going nowhere. He didn't have a clue about who killed the old detective. He lifted his brows.

'You said fresh cherry pie, young lady?'

'That I did. If you don't fill up on beans.'

'Sign me up for two orders of everything.'

They had just left the office when a deputy sheriff ran up and waved at West.

'You David West?'

'Right.'

'Sheriff wants to see you right away. There's been another murder. Two slugs into the back of this guy's head while he sat at his desk.'

7

The deputy, who West hadn't met, told him about it on the way to the store half way down the block from the agency.

'An accountant shot in the back of the head. Looks like there was no struggle. Nothing upset or out of place. Sheriff said it looked exactly like the Kramer killing three months ago.'

They went upstairs and into a small office. Sheriff Ramsden motioned West into the room from where he had stopped at the door.

'Take a look, West. An exact copy of what happened to Mr Kramer. Again it's two shots, look like small caliber of some kind. Dead in his chair. Doc Eaton is coming. The woman downstairs in the shop said she hadn't seen this man today. Could have happened last night. He's gone stiff already.'

The doctor bustled into the room with his small black bag. He tried to lift one of the dead man's hands. It wouldn't budge from where it lay on the desk top. He looked at the sheriff.

'Yep, you're right. He's been dead twelve, maybe sixteen hours. Undertaker is gonna have his hands full. Two shots to the back of the head. You don't need me here anymore. I'll make out a report. Oh, what's his name?'

'Barney Nelson,' the sheriff said. 'He's an accountant and about as harmless as a bunny rabbit. Why would anyone want to kill him?'

'Something he was working on, maybe,' West said. 'What's that paper under his hands?'

The paper turned into a half dozen pages of an accounting of the business of the Grossamer Hotel.

'Sheriff, I'm sure you'll explore all the suspects, like angry husbands, failed businesses, like that. I'm wondering if this has anything to do with Mr Kramer? Could Mr Nelson have been handling some large money operation here in town that nobody knew anything about? Did he do any work for the lawyer Charest?'

'You're asking the wrong person,' the sheriff said. 'But I'm giving you permission to look through the files here and see what you can find he was working on that might have some bearing on who killed him. Fair enough?'

'More than fair, Sheriff Ramsden. I'll start right now, or just as soon as the undertaker gets his work out of here.'

A half hour later the undertaker and his helpers had carried the stiff body down the stairs and into a buggy to take it away. West checked over the place in general. No litter, nothing in trays or stacks of papers. Everything had been filed neatly. In the top drawer he found a diary where Nelson had kept a running account of each client and how much time he spent on the accounting. Most of them were twice a year. Some once a month. He went through the book quickly and didn't find Charest's name.

After another hour's search he did a review of two tall file cabinets that had dozens of file folders in them all neatly indexed and labeled. The first name he looked for was Charest. It wasn't there. However there were no files at all starting with the letter C. Strange. He checked farther along and found a file marked 'Kramer Detective'. Inside were balance sheets evidently on a six month basis, showing the balance sheets of the firm and the financial position.

Back at the detective office he found Susan waiting for him.

'Anything?'

'Nothing to help. I was certain that the killing must be connected to your father's murder. But I haven't found any sign of it so far. Did Nelson do a lot of books for the business people in town?'

'He was the best. He even did a twice yearly audit on our books here at the agency. Not that we had a lot of money to keep track of.'

'I'm giving up on it for tonight,' West said. 'You think the beans are done by now?'

Susan smiled and headed for the door. 'Let's go take a look.'

The navy white beans were done without a crunch and the mashed potatoes and bacon gravy turned the meal into a feast followed by that fresh cherry pie with whipped cream topping.

West eased back from the table and watched Susan. All this and she could cook too. 'I don't think I've ever had bacon gravy before. It was great. If I ate like this every day I'd have to buy larger pants every month. That was delicious. Now, solve our two murders and all will be right with the world. Or at least our little squib of it here in Colorado.'

Susan stopped putting away dishes and watched him; her pert face concerned for a moment, and then blossomed into a smile with her green eyes glinting. 'Cowboy, I think you like our little state.'

'I do, I do, only — '

'Only it isn't home.'

'Right. You see, I have some unfinished business back there on the East Coast I need to take care of.'

'But not right yet?'

'Not until we dig out the man who killed your dad.'

'You need to get away from the case for a while. How about some dominoes? I bet I can whip you good on a game to five hundred.'

'Count every end and play on all doubles and count nothing but multiples of five?'

'You've got it. Help me clear the table and we'll get the game going. I haven't beaten anyone at dominoes since . . . well for quite a while.'

After an hour he knew she was good. She played well, counted big numbers and watched his play so she figured out some of the tiles he had left. Twice she blocked his play and made him go to the bone pile, then went out and tallied up his remaining dominoes. She won the first game 523 to 325. She won the second game 515 to 413.

'Enough, you're the champ. Now I need to get some sleep so I can dig, dig, dig, as Rocky said tomorrow. Don't know where I'll dig but I've got to come up with a suspect or two.'

She walked him to the door, then stood close to him and looked up. 'You haven't paid for losing those two games,' she said.

He frowned. 'Paid?'

'You owe me a kiss goodnight.'

West grinned, bent and kissed her cheek. She shook her head. 'Doesn't count, not a multiple of five. She held his face in both hands and kissed his lips lightly then with more force and came away.

'Now, your debt is paid. Maybe you'll win the next time.'

West chuckled, told her goodnight and went out the door.

* * *

The next morning he waited at the agency for her to arrive at 8.15. She handed him a key. It was for the real lock on the door, a tumbler type with a round face and years away from the skeleton key type most doors still used.

'You should have a key so you don't have to wait. Or so you can come in when I'm not here.'

He sat at his desk, drawing squares and circles on a pad of paper. At last he stood and went out without saying a word. He walked down one side of the long Main Street and back up the other. He hardly noticed the stores or the people. Then he turned and saw someone behind him. The boy was maybe ten or eleven, with clean trousers, good shoes, and a shirt tucked in his pants held up by suspenders. As soon as West turned, the boy looked away. West walked on a dozen steps and watched behind him. The boy was following him, using the same type walk West had, the same arm swing, and the same even paced steps. The boy held his arms the same way West did and turned quickly and looked away as soon as he saw West watching him.

West turned suddenly and walked back to the boy. For a moment the kid panicked, almost ran, then took one step away and stopped. This time he looked directly at West. There was no smile on his face. That's when West noticed that his face had been scrubbed to a pinkish clean. His hair was parted and combed, his hands even looked clean.

'What's your name, young man?'

The boy turned away and shook his head.

'I won't hurt you, just wondered why you're following me.'

He looked at West a moment, and then turned away.

Twice more West walked a short distance and stopped and talked to the boy, but he wouldn't say a word.

A woman in her forties passing by saw the scene and motioned to West.

'Sir, that's the Henderson boy. He

won't hurt a muskrat. He had a real shock two years ago and his mother says he hasn't said a word since then. What a shame. He's a good boy.'

West stopped in the Thompson General Store and bought a dime's worth of penny candy. Back on the street he sat in a chair next to the store and motioned for the boy to sit in the one next to him. Slowly the boy edged up and sat. West handed him the small sack of candy. The boy's eyes went wide. He looked at West and took out one piece and handed the bag back to West. The detective grinned, stood and dropped the sack on the boy's lap as he walked down the street toward the agency. Inside he told Susan about his new friend.

'Oh, yes, the Henderson boy. Two years ago he saw his father shot to death in a robbery in his store. His mother says that he hasn't said a word since then. A real shame. Such a nice young boy. He's about twelve. He used to follow Dad around. I don't think he's followed anyone else since then. You have an admirer.'

'Can't hurt.' He stood and walked to the window. 'I've been thinking.'

'About time,' she jibed.

'Yeah, true. I saw that country they bought. Bad scrabble, good for nothing gullies, rocks, shale and hills and ravines. It has to be some kind of mineral up there they are interested in. If not silver or gold, what else is there? Magnesium, asphalt, coal, iron ore, copper, even salt. It has to be some kind of a mining operation. Or it could be oil, but this doesn't seem like the kind of land where oil seeps out of the ground. Who in town is an ex-miner or somebody who knows the most about digging things out of the ground?'

8

David West had spent most of the morning trying to get a handle on the facts about the killing. There wasn't much. He gave up about ten o'clock and walked the street for a while. It didn't take long to go up one side of the small town's main street and down the other. For a second he stiffened. Someone was following him. He turned casually, his right hand near his six-gun's butt on his thigh.

West grinned and relaxed. It was Billy Henderson, the 12-year-old kid who wouldn't talk. West watched him a moment. Billy had stopped when West did. He didn't look directly at West, rather to one side, but he knew every move West made. West walked slowly into the Springs General Store. The boy waited on the boardwalk. West bought a nickel's worth of hore-hound candy. He took the sack out and popped one of the candies in his mouth, then handed the sack to Billy. The boy looked up directly at West. He blinked and his face worked for a moment, then he reached out and took the sack. He held the small paper bag but didn't reach into it.

'Well now, I guess we're making some progress.' West held out his hand. 'I'm David West, and you're Billy. Good to meet you, Billy.' Slowly the boy's hand came up and touched the much larger palm, then went quickly back to his side.

West nodded, turned and headed for the Springs Livery. He had one more suspect to check out, but it would take a ride. It was downstream on the creek that never would become a river to the Demarest ranch. He rented a horse from Fred Ihander and headed south. The stream that came out of the springs perked up a bit with more inflow, then evened out at about ten feet across and meandered down the small valley.

The Demarest ranch was four miles

south, in a small pocket of range grass and some stark, bare cliffs. The ranch house wasn't much, two rooms, West figured and no curtains on the one window, which meant there probably wasn't a woman involved.

He had seen fifty head of cattle, mixed yearlings and cows on his ride in. There was no corral, one small barn, and a well house. He saw a saddled horse tied to a hitching post just outside the cabin door. West called out as he rode up.

'Hello, the Demarest ranch. You've got a visitor.'

The screen door swung open and a man about thirty came out carrying a six-gun in his hand. His range clothes were a bit ragged and dirty. He was medium sized and lean. His face was half tan and half white, showing that he rode a lot in the sun with his wide brimmed hat on. He stared at West for a minute, and then snapped a shot from his .44 two feet from the mount's feet.

'You ain't company. I know who you

are. So turn around and ride back to town before you regret it.'

'Mr Demarest. So you've got a temper and a gun and probably a grudge against the man who sent you to prison. You hated the sheriff, didn't you?'

'Oh yeah. He stole five years right out of my life. I didn't do no more than lots of men did, but he nailed me for the job. Yeah I was furious with the sheriff.'

He fired again and the horse stepped three feet to the side away from the sound of the gun.

'OK, one question. Did you kill him?'

'The sheriff wasn't stupid. He wouldn't let me walk behind him with a gun on me. Now lite out before I get really mad.'

West tipped his hat, turned the horse around and walked the mount out of the ranch yard. On the ride back to town he thought it through. Demarest was right, the sheriff would remember him and not let him even come into the office. Demarest was still angry, but not killing angry. Scratch one more suspect.

Back in town, West didn't go to the hotel. He had a quick late lunch at the Nugget Cafe, and then talked to Susan at the office.

'You said the lawyer, Charest, was as crooked as a wind-blown pine tree?'

'More than that, sneaky, under-handed, and smiling all the time with his sweet talk and glad handing. He's a menace.'

'So if there was a big money operation going on anywhere around he would know about it?'

'He'd be in on it, probably calling the shots.'

'So, I'll tail the lawyer man for a couple of days and see what he does. Sounds, reasonable. Heaven knows I don't have anything else to go on.'

Susan nodded and watched him. Her face lit up when she saw him look at her. 'Would your overloaded social calendar have room in it for a home cooked fried chicken supper tonight? Mashed potatoes and gravy, fresh baked rolls, stuffing, and some new carrots?'

'Tempting, but I'm going to be shadowing the good Mr Charest no matter what he does or where he goes. Is he married?'

Susan laughed and he liked the way it brightened her face. 'Oh my, yes. The good Mr Charest has little time for marriage, but the gossip is he has lots of time for other women. His wife has to know about his philandering.'

'Figures. And if I may I'll take a rain check on that home cooked supper.'

'Done.'

He stood and she frowned. 'You're still wearing that gun?'

'I am. Seems like for the time being I may need a little protection.' He waved and stepped out the door onto the boardwalk and headed for the lawyer Charest's office. West walked by the place once and saw the lawyer in a chair behind his desk. So, he had him in his sights, where did he sit and wait?

He went across the street to the Nugget Café, only two doors down. He got a cup of coffee and sat at a window table and went over the current copy of the *Junction Springs Record.* Anything that moved across the street and anyone who went in or out of the Charest law office caught West's attention. It must be a slow day for the lawyer. Only one person came out of the office while he watched the rest of the afternoon. He had three cups of coffee and a piece of cherry pie and that spoiled his supper.

He followed the lawyer to the Stage Coach Restaurant on the corner of Third Street and Main. West had roast beef for his supper while he watched Charest put away a full pound steak supper. After the meal Charest looked in at the Laughing Lady Saloon. He had a quick beer at the bar and left.

It took him ten minutes to walk to a house near the far end of Main Street. It was the best house on the block and looked as if it had been recently painted white with a soft blue trim. A front yard with grass and roses completed the picture.

By ten o'clock the last light in the Charest house blinked out and West walked back to the hotel. It had been a long day. He closed and locked his second floor room, then wedged the back of the straight chair under the door handle as was his custom, and soon went to sleep.

The next morning in the Kramer Detective Agency office, West gave up on the idea of following Charest.

'It could be days before he meets anyone or anything happens that I could get a clue about what's going on. There must be a better way.'

He was filling his coffee cup for the second time when Rocky walked into the office with a sly grin. He groaned as he eased down in his favorite chair and motioned to the coffee pot. West brought him a cup, black and hot. Rocky pulled off his shoes and massaged his feet.

'Yes sir, nothing beats a good cup of coffee come morning,' Rocky said. 'Just about nothing.'

West grinned at the older man who was so brimming over with delight and a secret he couldn't hold much longer. West stood and looked at the door.

'Think I'll stroll down to the bank and see if money really does grow on trees.'

Susan smiled and sipped her coffee. Both of them were now staring at Rocky. He squirmed on his chair a moment, had another drink of his coffee and put it down on the edge of West's desk.

'OK, you beat it out of me. It was my little secret. Now the whole town will know.'

West chuckled. 'Hey older than Methuselah, you're gonna be the one outside running down Main Street with me peppering .44 slugs at your heels unless you tell us what you found out when you trailed Ellis Younger, the mayor's son.'

'Dang. How'd you know?' He harrumphed a minute then nodded. 'Oh, yeah. That was my assignment, wasn't it?' He stopped and looked at the little stove. 'Any more coffee?'

Susan threw a wadded up piece of paper at him. 'Not a drop until you tell us what you dug up. Out with it.'

Rocky rubbed his hand over his face, then his thinning hair on top, and when his hand came down he grinned as wide as a haymow door.

'This Ellis Younger is quite a character. I watched him grow up. Does a lot of running around town on all sorts of errands.' He sipped his coffee letting the drama build. 'Well he hit two poker games right after lunch. I kind of waited around in the background with a beer. He went into two stores and I hung around the front or across the street until he came out. Then he went back to the old land office where he and his dad sell houses now and estates and land and such. Not five minutes after he went in, I saw this classy looking lady walk up to the door and go inside. She didn't come out for some time. I walked by and didn't see anyone in the office through the window. So, I went in the door making considerable noise. Just as I got inside, Ellis comes out of the small back room. His hair is mussed and his tie is half off.'

'No law against that,' Susan said.

'Then a minute later this classy woman comes out the same door. Her hair was mussed and her white blouse only had the top two buttons fastened and it was pulled out loose from her long skirt. She kind of held the cloth together with her hand and said something to Ellis about not being ready to buy a new house just yet and hurried out the door.

'I pretended not to notice and asked Ellis how much my old house was worth. He told me and I left.'

'Who is the woman?' West asked.

Susan laughed softly and shook her head. 'Some hanky panky if I've ever seen it,' she said. She and West moved in front of Rocky and stared down at him where he sat in the chair.

'Come on, you wise old owl,' Susan

said. 'Who was the woman?'

'Oh, didn't I say? Classiest lady in town, dresses nicely, hair always fixed, probably even got on rouge and nails all polished.'

'Who is she?' Susan demanded.

Rocky grinned and sipped his coffee. 'Thought I told you. She's Lillian Charest, wife of our loophole lawyer.'

Susan looked stunned for a moment. Then she scowled. 'That could be nothing but a little petting in the office. Is there more?'

'Fact is there is, but isn't it about time for lunch?'

'No, Rocky, you just came in. Not even nine o'clock yet.'

'Oh. Well, there is more to the story. I knew last night was city council meeting. Charest is the city attorney, so he would be there. I took a chance and found a nice comfortable place to sit and watched the Charests' back door just as it was getting dark. Blamed if I wasn't right. Ellis came slipping down the alley and looked both ways, then hurried up to the Charest back door and let himself in.'

'So?' Susan said.

'A gentleman caller when her husband is out of the house. They have no kids underfoot. Figures.' Rocky said.

'When did Ellis leave?' West asked.

'Not until after 9.30. The city council starts its meetings at seven and is always done by 9.30. Ellis had it timed out almost to the minute.'

Susan reached for the little blue hat she'd been wearing lately and headed for the door.

West held up both hands. 'Wait a minute. You're probably going right down to the younger Mrs Younger and spill the beans about Ellis's sleeping around.'

'Absolutely. She should know.'

West nodded. 'Oh, yes she should know, but maybe not just yet.'

Susan frowned and cocked her head to one side.

'What are you saying, West? Out with it.'

'I used to go hunting with my father. He would always tell me to walk quietly but carry a big gun.' He looked around but the puzzlement was plain on their faces. 'I think we've got a big gun here. We know that Mrs Charest is bedding young Mr Younger. We think that Mr Charest is up to some kind of a scheme that may have led to murder. Why don't we talk to Mrs Charest, tell her we know she's having an affair with the younger Mr Younger and suggest that we'll keep her dirty little secret if she does some snooping around her husband's affairs and try to find out who he's talking with and what they are planning?'

'That is the most sneaky, unprofessional thing I've ever heard of,' Susan said scowling. Her scowl changed to a grin. 'And I love it. You have to do the talking.'

Rocky chuckled. 'Bless me, Father, but I think the boy has a whammer of an idea here. Don't see what it can hurt. If she finds out something, we're belly deep in clover. If she doesn't, don't matter one quarter of a good cow's morning milking.'

Susan looked at West. 'I should have you change into a suit and a tie, but I guess the jeans and blue shirt will do. I mean, you're representing Kramer Detective Agency.'

'How old is Mrs Charest?' West asked.

'She's about thirty,' Susan said. 'Ellis Younger is just past twenty-one.'

'Older woman, younger man,' West said. 'That will work for us too.'

Susan looked at the wind up clock on her desk. 'Just past ten o'clock. Mrs Charest should be up by now.'

West rubbed his jaw. 'A suit would be good, but I don't have one. Several in Boston but that doesn't help.' He took out the small notebook he carried in his back pants pocket and wrote down something. 'I'll consult my notebook when I'm talking with her,' he said. He looked at Susan and Rocky. 'Hey, this has to work. I'll give it my best shot.'

Ten minutes later West knocked on the door of the Charest house. He waited, and then knocked again, four serious sounding raps with his knuckles on the wooden panel.

A moment later the door edged open four inches and blue eyes looked out.

'Yes, what do you want?'

'Mrs Victor Charest? I have something to talk to you about. May I come in?'

'Who are you?'

'My name is David West, and I work with Susan Kramer.'

'I know her.' She hesitated, then backed away and opened the door. He stepped inside and she closed the door. She wore a blue housecoat and her shoulder length blonde hair had been carefully combed and touches of rouge applied to her cheeks and her lips. She was about five feet four inches and on the slender side.

'You said you had something to talk about.'

'Yes, could we sit down? I don't want

you fainting dead away on me.'

'My goodness, that sounds serious. Yes, in the parlor.'

They went through a door and sat on an overstuffed couch that faced the front windows.

'Now, what is it?'

'Mrs Charest, you must understand that I'm working with Susan trying to find out who murdered her father. No, I don't think that you or your husband did it. There is something strange going on in town with some sections of land nearby being bought. Your husband is part of that. We need to know what it is.'

'I know nothing of my husband's business. Even if I did — '

'Mrs Charest,' he said cutting her off, his voice harsh and demanding. 'We know that you're having an affair with Ellis Younger. We know that yesterday afternoon you were in his office with him alone. We know that he was at your house last night from about 7.30 to 9.30.'

Her expression went from stern to surprise, then she held her face with both hands and she cried silently. When she looked up tears ran down her cheeks.

'How in the world did you know?'

'His wife said she suspected him, so it was our job to find out if Ellis was having an affair.'

She gave a big sigh and looked out the window. 'So now I suppose you'll tell the newspaper and there'll be a big story and Victor will divorce me and I'll have to leave town.'

'Not at all, Mrs Charest. We plan on telling no one. Only three of us know about it. You can break off the affair at once and no one will ever need to know.'

She scowled as she looked at him. Distrust and anger pinching her pretty face. 'And what is it going to cost me? You aren't here for the simple joy of humiliating me.'

'That's true, Mrs Charest. We want you to find out what your husband is doing buying up land outside of town. We need to know why he's doing this and if that process had anything to do with the death of Mr Kramer.'

'You think Victor shot Mr Kramer?'

'No, he's too smart for that. But we need to know what this land buy is all about. Will you help us?'

She recovered a little and took another deep breath. Slowly she nodded, 'Is there any way that I can bargain with you, Mr West?' West couldn't help but stare at her.

'Good try, Mrs Charest, you are beautiful but you're not in a bargaining position. You must agree to find out what your husband is doing in this land grab, or we'll tell him about your infidelity. You have three days to get the job done.' He turned and walked to the parlor door where he stopped and turned back. 'I'll be back in three days at ten o'clock to have your report.'

West turned and walked out the door. He realized he was sweating only when he hit the cooler air of the

Colorado morning outside. He shook his head and laughed. He saw how the younger Mr Younger didn't stand a chance if she set her cap for his attention. Now, they would have three days to work on any other leads while they waited for Mrs Charest to dig up what the land buys were all about. If she could do it.

9

All the next day David West went over what they knew about the Kramer murder, and everything else connected with the killing in any way. The four former convicts seemed as pure as a baby's first breath. He had almost nothing to go on, except the parcels of land changing hands.

On the second day of Mrs Charest's investigation, he discovered that two more plots of land near the town had been sold. He found out when he made a casual check with the county recorder.

'Oh, Mr West, I have some news for you. Two more plots of land were recorded today. They sold out near the other new ones we talked about.'

'The same company listed as the owner?'

'Right, the Warren-Hall Land Company of Denver.'

'What in blazes is going on?'

'Beats me,' the recorder said. 'All I have to do is take down the facts and figures.'

'Corporation, you said it was the same corporation. Don't the owners of a corporation, at least the officers, have to be listed with the state? Some kind of a corporate state office?'

'Right. It's called the Colorado Corporation Office.'

'I bet you have an address for it.'

The clerk nodded and dug out the address, which West copied down. It was in Denver.

'Folks up there are right friendly,' the clerk said. 'You send them a wire and I reckon they'll send you back what you want to know right quick.'

West thanked the clerk and hurried over to the train station and the telegraph office. The woman clerk behind the counter looked over the wire West wrote out. She was in her forties, gray hair, wore spectacles perched on the end of her nose and watched him from brown curious eyes.

'Save a quarter by rewriting it a little,' the woman said. 'Just cut out the 'the's' and a couple of other words. Say the same thing. Want me to help?'

West nodded. The final version read: 'Please send me a collect wire with names and addresses of the officers of the Warren-Hall Land Company of 2243 Creek Street, Denver, Colorado.' He signed his name and Junction Springs, Colorado as his address.

'Good. That will be a dollar and eighty-five. Check back here any time this afternoon or tomorrow morning and you should have a reply.' She smiled. 'New in town, I'd figure. Hear you working with Susan. Nice girl, Susan. You be good to her.'

West said he would and wandered back to the street. He hated waiting around. He walked out a quarter of a mile to the edge of town and practiced shooting with his Colt. He missed the tree the first five rounds. Then his aim improved. He shot all but five rounds from his gunbelt loops, then took those out and reloaded the Colt, and walked back to the detective agency office.

He told Susan about the two more land buys.

'It's got to be minerals of some kind,' she said after sipping her coffee. 'But what in the world could it be?'

Rocky looked up from the *Denver Post* that came in on the train every morning. 'Got to be gold. Why all this fuss over anything less valuable?'

'Even salt is valuable,' West said. 'People who own the underground salt mines are making millions of dollars.'

'Not much chance of a dried up ocean out here,' Rocky said.

'We'll find out eventually,' West said. He waved at Susan. 'How long did Billy Henderson follow your dad around?'

'Six months or so. Dad got tired of it after a while, especially when Billy wouldn't talk. At the last he just tried to ignore him. Billy never caused any trouble.'

'I saw him watching the agency when

I came in. He must be waiting for me again.'

'I hear you've been feeding him candy,' Rocky said.

'Well, sure. Why not? How did you know?' He threw up his hands. 'The fancy small town telegraph. Everybody knows everything about everybody.'

'Except Lillian Charest and you know who,' Susan said. 'I wonder how she's coming along in her detective work for us?'

'Tomorrow I go to her house and find out,' West said.

Rocky heaved to his feet with a groan. 'It's hard growing old. Seventy-four tough years I been walking on these same feet. Should be able to trade in body parts for new ones. Like the salamander that grows a new tail when one gets snapped off.'

'You off to the usual?' Susan asked.

'Probably, if any of them old farts show up. Used to be we had three tables going at once. Now we're lucky if we get four players.' He waved at them and ambled out the door.

West looked at Susan with his brows up.

'Checkers. Some of the older men meet in the court house lobby every afternoon to play checkers. No money changes hands but the competition is fierce.'

'Is that where you learned to play so well?'

'Oh, no, that's for men only. My father taught me to play dominoes and checkers too, when things were slow around here.'

'Figures. Hey, is that invitation to supper still on tap? I could use a good home cooked meal after these cafe victuals for a week.'

'The table is still set. All we have to do is stop by the Ralston Butcher shop on the way home and pick up a whole chicken.'

'It's a date.' He nodded. 'Yes, I've decided that I like that green dress you're wearing. It picks up some of the color of your eyes.'

'Well, thank you. I decided now that I have a real staff, I should look more professional.'

A small boy pushed the door open and looked in.

'Is there a David West here?' he asked. West figured the kid was about ten.

'That's me, young man. Why?'

He took an envelope from behind his back and held it out.

'Telegram for you, figured it was important and didn't want to wait for you to stop by.'

'It's collect,' West said. 'Can I trust you to get two dollars and eighty-five cents back to that nice lady at the telegraph office?'

'You sure can. That nice lady is my grandma and she'll switch my bottom good if'n I don't bring back the money.' West fished three dollar bills out of his wallet and gave them to the boy who gave him the envelope. 'Tell your grandma that the change is your charge for delivery.'

'Yes sir,' the boy squealed and hurried out the door.

West told her about his wire to the state office.

'Fast service for anyone in Denver,' Susan said. 'Well, open it, let's see who the officers of that corporation are.'

They read the wire together. The first name was the president listed as Victor R. Charest, vice president, Pelton Younger, the mayor. Neither of them knew the other three men named. Those three all had Denver addresses.

'At least we're making progress,' West said. 'We know who the locals are who are pushing this, we just don't know why.'

He paced the office trying to make sense of it all. When he stopped in front of Susan he had an idea.

'I'm going to see Lillian Charest and tell her about this corporation her husband is heading and the land they are buying. It might help her find out something for us.'

'Not the front door,' Susan said.

'There are too many idle eyes up in that section of town. Try her back door.'

'Good idea. You're not only pretty as a nosegay of bluebells, you're smart too.'

'Thank you, kind sir,' Susan said but she couldn't help but blush just a little. West hurried out the front door.

He turned off the north part of Main Street a half block before he came to the Charest house, and worked his way slowly up the alley. Not much cover there, but not many eyes either. When he came to the Charest house, he walked up to the back door and knocked sharply on the wood. He waited twice as long as he usually did between knocks. Then he pounded with the side of his fist on the door six times.

A second later he heard a screech of someone inside, and then steps and a moment later the door opened. Lillian Charest peered out and then swung the door open.

'Inside before someone spots you.' She waited for him to step in then closed the door. 'What now? You said I had until tomorrow.'

'Right, you do. I just learned that your husband is president of the corporation that is buying up the land around here. The mayor is the vice president. Knowing this might give you an advantage in talking with your husband. That's it I'll go now. And find out what he is doing, or you may end up in divorce court.'

'I did find out something. Do you want to hear it?'

'Yes.'

'Victor said he might have a big surprise for me in a week or so. Until then he had to keep everything as quiet as possible. He didn't say it was about the land, he never mentioned it or the corporation you talked about. He just said he had to keep a lid on it, was the way he put it, for another week.'

West smiled grimly. 'All right, we've got a start. Now tonight use your wiles and tease him until he'll tell you everything. Get him worked up and then deny him for a while. Find out what they are doing with that land.'

'Yes, it might be fun denying him for a while, for as long as I can stand it. Talk to me tomorrow morning about ten.'

West left the house and went out the alley the long way, then walked back to the office. It was nearly five o'clock when he got there. Susan was starting to close up.

'Thought you forgot about our dinner date.'

'Not a chance.' He told her what Lillian Charest had told him.

'A week? How can a week make any difference to those barren hills and cliffs and gullies?'

'Got me. Let's hope she can find out tonight.'

'She's going to use her womanly wiles on her husband to get him to talk? I hope it works.'

'So do I. Now, pretty lady, you said something about buying some chicken for our dinner.'

* * *

Two hours later West helped Susan with the dishes. He was on dry.

'I told you that you didn't have to do that,' Susan said.

'Hey, I pay my way. If I do a good job I might get invited back. The chicken dinner was fantastic. I'll gain ten pounds.'

Susan's round face broke into a glorious smile and she looked up at him. 'That just might happen, you getting invited back, you never can tell. But I don't want all of our other employees to get jealous.'

'Hey, technically I'm not an employee. I'm more like an unpaid intern learning the business. What other employees?'

'Rocky.'

'Yeah, there's always Rocky. When the dishes are done do we play dominoes or poker?'

'I'm not much good at poker.'

'Good, we'll play poker, got a big box of kitchen matches?'

They played poker, mostly five card draw, for two hours and when they stopped she had most of the matches. He had written down a chart showing her what hand beat what hand.

On the last hand she laid down a full house to his pair of aces and grinned. 'Hey, looks like I win again. I like this game. We'll have to play for pennies next time.'

'With real money on the table you won't take so many chances.'

'Wait and see.'

At the front door she held his hand and then pulled him toward her. 'Would it be all right if I asked you for a good hug? It's been a long time and I really like hugs.'

He wrapped both arms around her and hugged her tightly, lifted her off the floor and twirled her around once and brought her down to a soft landing. He released her slowly but she held on. At last she backed away.

'Wow, now that's what I call a friendly hug.'

West grinned and opened the door. 'Anytime, but probably not at the office.'

She nodded and waved as he went out the door.

* * *

A short time later he eased into his second floor room at the Grossamer Hotel and looked out the window at Main Street. It was a little after 9.30, but most of the town was shuttered and dark. He saw a figure sitting in a captain's chair in front of the hardware store across the street and down two stores. There were four chairs there for the weary and loafers. Strange that there was someone there tonight. The man looked at the hotel from time to time and as far as West could tell he checked this second story window where West stood. He lit the coal oil lamp on the dresser and quickly went back to the side of the window and checked the man in the chair. He had been looking the other way. When he scanned the hotel windows he came down on all fours of the chair, stood, and hurried up the street.

West had grown a little paranoid since Boston and now he shivered when the man left the chair. They knew he was in his room. Would that mean he would have company tonight, deadly company?

He gathered up his gear, threw it in his bag and took everything he owned from the room and went down the hall trying doors along the way. He checked one door that was locked. His key opened it quickly and he found no one had rented it. He put down his gear and his bag, slid the straight backed chair under the door handle and eased down on the bed without lighting the lamp.

For an hour he tried to get to sleep, but something kept him wide awake. Preservation he decided it was called. He looked at his pocket watch in the flare of a match and saw that it was just after midnight. He got up and began pacing the small room. He hadn't undressed, not even taken off the cowboy boots he had bought three days before.

He was about to look at his watch again when a shattering explosion echoed down the hall. He waited a moment, then pulled the chair away from the door, and edged it open. Down the hall toward his room of record he saw a pall of smoke and noted the distinctive smell of dynamite. The door to his registered room hung in the hallway by one hinge. Smoke and the acrid smell of explosives drifted up the hall. Doors popped open along the hall.

'What was that?' a man in a nightshirt asked.

'Somebody blew the dickens out of that room down there,' another man wearing an undershirt said.

West stepped into the hall and eased down toward the room.

The night clerk charged up the stairs and ran to the room.

'My, somebody blew the place to pieces!' he shouted. 'Who would do something like that?' He frowned. 'Was someone in the room?' He looked at West. 'Can you bring a lighted lamp from your room? There might be a severely injured man in there.'

West brought the lamp and the clerk held it high as they went into the room. Most of the smoke and fumes had been blown out the window by that time. The window was shattered and glass sprinkled the entire room. The bed had been blasted apart, the bed boards scattered on the floor and the mattress and blankets on the bed ripped and torn into tatters. The dresser had been blasted against the hall wall and shattered into a dozen pieces. There was no sign of the small wash stand and the porcelain wash bowl and pitcher.

'Lift up the mattress for me can you, sir?' the clerk asked.

West pushed the mattress to one side and lifted it.

The clerk let out a long sigh. 'Well, at

least there doesn't seem to be a body here. Thank goodness for that. Maybe he hadn't come in yet. What in the world would have caused this?'

West pointed to the glass inside the room. 'Somebody threw a dynamite bomb from the street through the window. That's why the glass is on the inside of the room. Two, maybe three sticks of dynamite on a foot long fuse would have done it.'

'Thank our lucky stars that the walls didn't fall down or the third floor cave in. We'll have a big clean up in the morning. Who would want to throw a bomb into my hotel?' The clerk left, scratching his head and carrying the lamp as he went down the steps.

West went back to the new room he had moved into. He locked his door, put the chair under the handle, and lay down with all of his clothes and boots on. Who had tried to kill him this time? He must be getting close enough to the plotters to make them nervous. He'd have to be especially careful from now on. He'd move to a different room every night.

* * *

When morning came, West wasn't sure if he had gone to sleep that night or not. He brushed off his clothes, put on a clean shirt and made a stab at combing his hair.

Downstairs he told the room clerk that he had survived the bombing. He was down the hall when it happened. Said he was now in room 207. The clerk was still there from the night before and broke down when he saw West. He thought he had died in the explosion.

West got free of him after a few minutes and slipped out the side door to the Nugget Cafe for a stack of flapjacks and maple syrup. He sat in the back and kept his hat on the way the cowboys did only his was to partly hide his face. Someone was trying to kill him again and this time they seemed more deadly than before.

He went down a side street to the office and eased in behind his desk just as Susan came in. She hadn't heard about the bombing so he didn't tell her. Instead he scanned the *Junction Springs Record.* Ira Haines had put the land grab story on the front page. He recorded each of the large sales of land to the Warren-Hall Land Company but didn't have the officers of the corporation. West would tell him.

'Heading over to the newspaper office,' West told Susan. 'See what we can figure out on this land grab.'

She looked up from some papers her pretty face working into a frown. 'You're still carrying your gun?'

'Right. Somebody out there doesn't like me. I'm not going to play like a fish in a barrel for them.'

'Yes, I guess. I just wish all this violence would stop.'

'It will stop when we stop it,' West said.

* * *

Ten minutes later at the newspaper office he pushed his feet up on the edge of a desk and shook his head at Ira Haines.

'Don't think so, newspaperman,' West said. 'The men who bought up that land did it for a specific reason. That's what we have to find out. I walked some of those parcels. They look good for nothing but rabbits and a squirrel or two. No steer can live off it. No farmer could plant a crop. The only thing they are good for is mining and we have to figure out what kind of mining.'

'No gold out there that's for sure,' the red-headed editor and publisher said. 'I've talked to prospectors who have been walking those gullies and cliffs for twenty years. They say it just isn't right for gold or silver. Not a sign, no placer gold down the gullies that might have washed out of a mother lode. No mother lode. But if Charest and Younger are investing money in those parcels, there's got to be something valuable in them.'

'So what's left?' West asked. 'Copper, coal, cement, iron ore, sulphur, magnesium, phosphorous, lead, nickel, tin, maybe even salt? Must be something valuable in there or the big money wouldn't pony up the cash to buy it up.'

'Those parcels are no where near the rail line, so the rail folks didn't get any of it in a land grant.'

'How much is land out in there worth?' West asked.

'Don't know. Last I checked it was going for maybe a dollar an acre.'

'I asked the county recorder how many acres are involved in the six parcels,' West said. 'He figured it out for me. It's a little over four thousand acres. That's over six square miles of hills and gullies and dry hardscrabble.'

'Got to be mining of some sort. Mining. Reminds me of a story I never got.' Ira flipped through a notebook. 'Yeah, right here. Three months ago I read a story in the *Denver Post* about the federal government offering millions of acres of federal land here in

Colorado for ten cents an acre for mineral rights. That's a steal. They want to encourage mining. I put the clip in my future story file and never saw anything more about it. The sale was for mineral rights only and told how to qualify, how big the parcels were and where they are located. Why didn't I hear anything more about it?'

'Maybe you missed the story.'

'Not a chance. I go over the Post every morning as soon as the train brings it in.'

'Maybe that day's papers were lost on the train.'

'Not likely. I'd raise Cain.'

'Sounds promising. I'll wire the Post mining editor and see what he knows about the story. I should have an answer before supper time.'

Ira pointed a pencil at him. 'As soon as you find out, you come back and tell me. Thanks for helping me dig up that story I'd lost track of.'

At the telegraph office, West wrote out the query to the mining editor, listed his return address, and asked for a reply today if possible. The same gray-haired grandmother took the message. She read it, and then looked up at West.

'You trying to spoil that grandson of mine, giving him fifteen cents that way? Land of Goshen notion.' She smiled. 'I thank you. Little Jake was thrilled to have fifteen cents all his own. I'll get your charge on this in just a minute.'

After the wire was in the process of being sent down the telegraph lines, West hurried to the Kramer Detective Agency to tell them he might have found the key.

The front, door stood open. Inside two chairs had been tipped over, papers littered the floor. He heard a groan and looked behind his desk. Rocky lay on the floor holding his head. Blood seeped between his fingers. He looked up and saw West.

'Thank goodness you're here,' he said slowly as if thinking about each word.

10

J. Thurston Paine had started his search for the man he said must have killed the wonderful girl in Boston, Jane Poindexter. From Boston he went to New York and discovered a faint trail that led to Denver. Then he worked the route south checking out each small town and whistle stop for any sign of a man with a Boston accent. He had been at the search for two weeks and was determined to track down Douglas Johnson or whatever he called himself now.

For two more days J. Thurston Paine hit the small towns and showed the picture to everyone who would listen to him. When he found nothing, he moved on to the next small town on the train.

When he stepped down from the passenger car at the station in Junction Springs, he had little enthusiasm for the hunt.

The second hotel he stopped at was the best one in town. He spoke to the clerk behind the desk who was young, eager, wore spectacles, and had slicked back his unruly hair with pomade. To his surprise the clerk recognized the picture and said indeed the man was staying at that very hotel.

He learned the name Johnson was using, David West. His heart raced. So close.

Paine said he wanted to surprise his friend and the clerk said he could wait in the lobby. Paine moved over to the side of the lobby as far out of the main sight lines as possible and sat on a soft sofa. He had his travel bag beside him. It was almost more than he could do to sit still. To realize that he was so close. Should he show the local sheriff the Boston warrant he had for the arrest, or should he confront Johnson and take him back to Boston on his own? He opened his bag and pulled out a small pistol. It was a .25 caliber and had an extremely short barrel. It fit nicely in his pocket. He pushed it out of sight in his front pocket and waited. He could wait there all day. Now his heart and soul were singing. Soon, terribly soon now, he would have Douglas Johnson, killer, in his power.

11

West felt a hatred he had never known before surge up in him. Coming after him was one thing. Targeting Susan to make him stop the investigation was altogether different. He took two deep breaths and got his voice under control.

'Rocky, are you hurt bad?'

'No, just scrapes and bruises, go after her. Go, go.'

'How long ago?'

'No idea.'

'How big were they? Young, older?'

'Don't know, masks on. Go, go.'

West sprinted down the hall to the back door and looked up and down the alley. No sign of her. A man painting the back of a store across the alley waved at West.

'Looking for the lady?'

'Yes.'

'Saw two masked men drag her out

of the door there and put her in a buggy and race away. One of them waved a gun at me and I ducked out of sight.'

'Which way did they go?'

The man pointed north up the alley.

'How long ago?'

The man took out a pocket watch. 'Maybe fifteen minutes. No more.'

West thanked him and looked at the dust of the alley. He could see the buggy wheel tracks plainly in the dirt and one horse's hoof prints between them. He started jogging up the alley following the prints. At the first cross street he lost the tracks in a dozen wide wheel wagon imprints and dozens of horse hoof tracks. They might have turned left and might have turned right. He couldn't tell. He ran back to the office and found a note pinned to the desk with a small knife.

'West. If you don't want Susan dead and buried, you best get out of town on the five o'clock train for Denver.'

West tore it down and went to look at Rocky. He was sitting in a chair holding a cloth to his bleeding head.

'Lunatic hit me with his six-gun,' Rocky said. 'Just patch it up and I'll be fine.'

'I'll go get Doctor Eaton to look at you. Bleeding like a stuck hog.'

'You've never seen a hog bleed, city boy. I'm fine.'

West looked up just as the Henderson boy ran into the office. He mumbled something and waved at West.

'Suuuuuu,' he stopped. 'Suuussss.' He stopped again. 'Suuusssan,' he said and his face broke into a smile. He waved and West followed him. In the alley Billy pointed to the buggy tracks and then north. He ran that way and West hurried along beside him.

They came to the cross street and Billy turned right and kept running. West could see no more buggy tracks, but Billy seemed to know where he was going. They went down a block that moved them out of the business part of the small town into a gaggle of houses spotted here and there on dirt streets laid out in a generally organized pattern.

A block later, Billy stopped beside one of the houses and crept up to the side of it so he could see around the wall. West did the same thing. Billy pointed at the house next door. There was a hand lettered for sale sign on the front door. Weeds had grown up in the front yard and there were no shrubs or flowers around it. West figured that no one had lived in the house for some time.

'Susan,' Billy said, pointing at the house.

'Susan is in that house?' West asked.

Billy nodded.

'Did you see the two men who brought her here in the buggy?'

Billy nodded.

'Did you follow them from the office?'

'Yyyyyyy yes.' Billy said.

West looked at the house again. There were no windows on this side.

He guessed that there were four, maybe five rooms in the place. He could get to the side of the house and not be seen if the men were inside. Would they have an outside lookout? He thought not.

'Billy, you stay here. I'm going to go get Susan.' He drew his six-gun, swung out the cylinder and put a sixth round in the empty chamber, then pushed the cylinder back in place.

West ran to the side of the house holding the weapon in front of him. If these men had hurt Susan he would kill them. He thought about it a moment and said 'yes' softly. Then he edged to the front of the house and looked around. He could see a front door and windows on both sides of it. If he crawled he could move under the closest window and get to the door without being seen. Would the door be locked? Probably not since they wouldn't expect any pursuit.

He dropped to his knees and holding the Colt ready, crawled under the window, and stood in front of the door.

He tested the door knob trying to turn it. It didn't move. Locked. He took two steps back and jumped at the door kicking out hard with his right boot.

The cheap lock snapped, the door jolted open, West landed on his feet, and charged into the room. A man sitting on a couch in the front room snarled and grabbed at his six-gun. West fired the Colt. The round hit the man in the shoulder and the gun flew out of his hand.

A woman's scream echoed through the house. West darted forward, grabbed the dropped six-gun and ran through a door into the next room. Susan sat on a bed that had fallen down on the end.

Sitting on a chair next to her was a short man pulling off his shirt. He saw the gun and held up his hands where he sat. West moved up slowly watching the man carefully. When he came close enough he slammed the six-gun down on the kidnapper's head. The man's eyes glazed, then shut, and he toppled off the chair unconscious.

Susan watched it all wide-eyed. She sat still, one hand coming up and wiping away a tear on her cheek.

'Susan, are you all right?'

She stared straight ahead. He knelt in front of her watching her closely. She blinked, looked at the man slumped unconscious on the floor, and then she began to cry. Softly at first, then the fear and terror came out in sobs as she reached out for West and he held her as she cried it out.

It was four or five minutes before the sobs subsided and she eased back from him and wiped away the tears.

'Better?' He asked.

She nodded.

West had heard movement in the front room and figured the other kidnapper had run out of the house. He wouldn't be hard to find. West stood.

'I'm going to see if the buggy is out back. Come with me.' She stood and they went into the front room, then out the door and around the house. The buggy with the horse still hitched to it was there. West handed her into the rig, then led the horse around to the front of the house. He carried the groggy kidnapper out and dumped him on the floor of the buggy. Then he got in and drove up near the next house.

'Billy,' West called. 'Want a ride?'

Billy ran out to meet them.

* * *

An hour later, West had dropped the kidnapper off at the sheriff's office and suggested that he send a deputy to wait at both the doctor's offices to see if anyone showed up with a gunshot wound. The missing kidnapper was about thirty, middle sized, with dark hair and a black inch-long beard.

Then West drove Susan to her house and went inside with her. Susan sat while West brewed her a pot of tea. They both had some and at last Susan could talk about it.

'That man hit Rocky. Is he hurt?'

West told her not badly hurt.

'That smaller man said all sorts of awful things to me. Told me what he was going to do. I was so frightened that I couldn't even move. He had his shirt off when he heard you break in. You saved my life, David West.'

He smiled. 'You are feeling better. I need to go take Rocky to see Doctor Eaton. I'll close up the office and come back and cook you some supper. Yes, I can do some cooking. I'll see what you have in your pantry.'

'I don't know if I want you to cook.'

'Is there someone I can talk to about staying with you here tonight? I don't want you to be alone.'

She wrinkled her brow in a mini frown and at last looked up.

'Yes, Amy Wilbur. She lives just two houses down. She lives with her mother and works at the bank. She should be home by now. Ask her.'

An hour later, West had all the arrangements made. Amy came down and would make supper for the two of them. He went back to the office and told Rocky what happened, then prodded Rocky into going to the doctor for some stitches in his forehead, and then got him home. He made sure Rocky was settled down then headed for the hotel to check to see if he had any messages. He started to go in the side door when he looked through the glass and stopped short.

There sitting in the lobby was J. Thurston Paine from Boston. How in the devil had he found him? And so quickly. West looked at his key box and saw some messages. West found a small boy and gave him a quarter to go in and get his messages from the room clerk.

'Show him the quarter I gave you and he'll let you bring the things out to me,' West told the boy. He did and a few minutes later came back with two white envelopes. One of them was from Lillian Charest. He read it:

'Mr West. I can't talk to you any more. My husband figured out I was pumping him for answers about his land deal. He's sending me to Denver to my sister's house for two weeks, so I can't find out anything else. I've done all I can. Please don't tell anyone about my grievous mistake. I trust you.' It was signed Lillian Charest.

The other message was about his 'brother' who was waiting for him in the lobby. West went back to the county jail. The kidnapper had recovered from his blow to the head but wouldn't tell the sheriff who hired him to do the job.

Sheriff Ramsden talked quietly to the man through the jail cell bars.

'Amos, you told us your name was Amos. I don't know how much somebody paid you to kidnap Miss Kramer but it wasn't enough. You're here on a charge of kidnapping. Did you know that in Colorado now we can hang you for kidnapping? True. The judge can give you life in prison or hang you. Usually it's hanging. Cost too much to keep you in prison. We've got three witnesses. The man painting in the alley, Rocky, and Billy Henderson. You might as well tell us, Amos. You're a dead man either way.'

He still wouldn't talk.

Sheriff Ramsden shrugged. 'Up to you, Amos. You're on our dry routine. No food or water until you talk. Usually it takes three days. You might break the record. We'll just wait and see.'

While West was there a deputy brought in a man with a black beard. He had a bandaged shoulder due to a gunshot wound. West recognized him at once as the other kidnapper. He told the sheriff.

'Told the doc his six-gun went off when he dropped it,' the deputy said. 'This one is a talker. I'd figure him for no more than two days on the dry schedule.'

West went on to the train depot and the telegraph office. A different clerk sorted through the telegrams and found one for West. He opened it there in the office and read it.

'Mr West. Yes, we ran stories on the opening of new parcels in your part of Colorado. You must not have seen them. It's called the Mining Incentive Law and the deadline for filing is in just a week. It opens up here too for closed sections of the state federal lands at the price of ten cents an acre for mineral rights. All privately owned land is exempt from this law. Any corporation or private person can buy up to 6,000 acres of mineral rights. All county clerks and county recorders in the state have the necessary forms and instructions how to claim these lands.'

West hurried to the county clerk and recorder's office before it closed.

'I've never heard of this law,' the clerk said. 'I certainly didn't get any forms or instructions about it.'

'Could someone stop such a mailing getting to you?' West asked.

'Could. Somebody in Denver could take our name off the mailing list for the material going out. Wouldn't be hard. For fifty dollars you can buy a lot of devilment in the state capital.'

'Could you wire the state and ask them to send a new batch of forms and applications to you on tomorrow's train?'

'Could and will,' the clerk said. 'A lot of people in town just might be interested in this mineral rights law.'

West walked back to Rocky's house. It was small and all he needed, he said. His wife of forty years had died nearly ten years ago, and he kept up the place the best he could. A neighbor lady come in once a week and cleaned and washed his clothes and did some cooking.

West knocked on the door and heard Rocky muttering as he shuffled to the front of the house.

'Oh, it's you. Thought it might be important.'

'Just me. I have a small problem and hoped you could help me.' West told the old detective about the Boston man waiting for him in the hotel.

'He could have a Boston warrant for my arrest. Yeah, I got in some trouble back there but it was all a mistake. All I need is a place to sleep tonight before I figure out how to deal with Mr J. Thurston Paine.'

Rocky waved him into a chair in the living room. 'Got into some trouble don't cut it, young feller. You tell me all about it, chapter and verse and then we'll figure out what to do.'

It was more than an hour later when West finished his tale about his beautiful lady friend and her murder.

'So who killed her?'

'I don't know. I have to go back to Boston soon to dig out the killer and clear my name. But right now, I'm on the track of another killer, and that comes first.'

'OK, you can stay here. Can you cook? Better than me, probably. Now let's figure out what to do to singe Mr Paine's tail feathers.'

* * *

The next morning, West slipped into the back door of the *Junction Springs Record* newspaper. He was still worried about the man from Boston being in town. Inside the alley door of the newspaper, he stopped and stared in amazement. The back shop had been completely trashed and ransacked. Paper, type cases, and cans of ink had been scattered everywhere.

12

He found Ira Haines on his knees in front of a tray of pied type. The individual metal letters on their narrow metal shafts were scattered over eight feet of the floor.

'Who did this?' West asked.

'Wish I knew. Only thing I can figure is the same people who are buying up the land.'

'We know who that is. What would this gain for them?'

'Maybe time,' Ira said. 'Gonna be two weeks before I can even think about getting out a new issue.'

'Time. I've heard something will happen in a week.' He told Ira about the deadline for filing on the ten cent land and that the county clerk could have the applications in on today's train.

'Even if they get here, what can we do?' Ira asked.

'Can you print up some broadsides? We could plaster them on every building in town.'

'Maybe. The twenty-four point tray isn't pied. I could set it in twenty-four point.'

'Is that bigger than newspaper type?'

'It's a quarter of an inch high, three times as high as body type in the paper.'

'Let's do it. I'll write it out and you set the type.'

A half hour later it was in type and Ira pulled a proof.

'NOTICE. MINERAL RIGHTS ARE NOW FOR SALE ON MANY PARCELS OF FEDERAL LAND NEAR HERE FOR TEN CENTS AN ACRE. SEE COUNTY CLERK FOR APPLICATIONS. DEADLINE IS THIS FRIDAY TO APPLY PRIVATE LANDS EXEMPT.'

Ira printed thirty of them on the proof press hand cranking each one. Then they took boxes of thumb tacks and began tacking the notices up on every building in town. There seemed to be an immediate reaction.

West checked at the county clerk's office.

'Yep, got a package of the applications in on the 8.10 train this morning. All set to go.' He looked up when a man came in.

'This where I get the application for that ten cent mineral rights land?'

'Indeed it is, sir.'

West grinned and walked out of the office. Then he thought about J. Thurston Paine. The Boston man was probably still at the hotel. He would have taken a room for the night. Back at the office, West wrote a note on a blank piece of paper:

'Hear you're hunting a man with a strange accent. One is holed up in an old ranch house about ten miles north of town. Figured you should know. A friend.'

He folded the note into an envelope and sealed it, then wrote on the outside. 'To the guy hunting a man with a strange accent.'

He gave the envelope to a boy and for a dime he delivered it to the desk clerk at the Grossamer Hotel. West pulled his hat down over his eyes and leaned back in a captain's chair outside the hardware store and watched the boy deliver the message. Then he waited for developments.

Ten minutes later a harried looking J. Thurston Paine rushed out of the hotel and marched up the street to the livery. West strolled along well behind him. At the stable, Paine evidently rented a horse and saddle and soon was on the quarter horse riding north up the trail. West laughed softly. Now he could work the whole town without any fear of running into Paine.

West moved where he could watch the lawyer's office. Charest probably was inside. He watched men reading the notices on the walls. Now and then one would turn in at the court house and the county clerk recorder.

A half hour after he started watching, a man hurried into the lawyer's office with one of the flyers in his hand. Two or three minutes later, Charest came storming out and headed straight for the mayor's property sales office. Charest left shortly, stopping to look at one of the flyers tacked to the hardware store wall. He continued back to his office and shut the door.

West walked into the mayor's business and saw him reading the flyer.

'Interesting, isn't it, Mr Vice President of the Warren-Hall Land Company.'

The mayor looked up quickly. 'Nothing illegal about my being an officer in a legal corporation.'

'No, but there is the problem of hiring a man to kill someone. Of hiring someone else to throw dynamite into a hotel room. And then of hiring two men to kidnap Susan Kramer. Those are three felonies under the law, Mr Mayor. The last one can get you hung when we convict you.'

Mayor Younger looked up shaking his head. 'Young man, I don't know what you're talking about. The corporation has done nothing illegal.'

West sat in a chair across the big desk and shook his head. 'True, nothing illegal about the corporation. Evidently you found some kind of mineral up in the hill land you had to protect from the government's cheap mineral rights offer, so you bought the land outright. So far you're free and clear.'

'So why are you accusing me . . . ?'

'Because you and Charest got nervous when I showed up and began asking questions about Kramer's killing. You or he and probably both of you, hired the two gunmen who came after me about the third day I was in town. A felony, Mr Mayor. Then there was the gunman Hondo who was supposed to kill me. He didn't. Again your hired hand. All the way to the kidnapping of Susan. You could get three hanging convictions in a matter of days. Do you want that to happen?'

Mayor Younger looked away. 'I didn't want to hurt anyone. They were only supposed to scare you.'

'That didn't work so you hired Hondo.'

'Charest's idea. I said no, but he did it anyway.'

'So, you're guilty of conspiracy to commit murder.'

'Now see here — '

'You're in too deep to get out free, Younger. If you testify against Charest, you could get a lighter sentence. Probably save yourself from the gallows.'

'I didn't really do anything . . . ' he stopped and sighed. 'I guess I did. Conspiracy. I didn't actually do it, just planned how to do it and — '

'Conspiracy to commit a kidnapping is a felony with a hanging sentence, Younger. Do you really want to risk that with a trial and a jury of townfolks?'

'A lot of these people hate me. I wouldn't stand a chance.'

'Then testify against Charest. Write out the whole thing about what happened and sign it.'

The mayor stood and walked to the

window, then back to his desk. He rubbed his face with his hands, then sat down and took out a pen and paper.

'Looks like I have no choice.'

'Start with who killed Mr Kramer.'

'That was Charest. He said it was in a moment of panic when he realized that Kramer knew about the government mineral rights deal and he was going to tell the newspaper man. He thought that would buy enough time for the deadline to pass.'

'You'd already started buying up the land?'

'Yes, almost three months before then when our Denver contact told us the law was coming.'

'Why did you buy the land?'

'To keep the mineral rights ourselves. We had stumbled on an old prospector who told us that he had found a good deposit of copper back in the hills. He told us where it was for five hundred dollars. Old coot showed Charest where it was and he had the ore assayed in Denver. It is copper and it's a rich deposit. The old guy drank himself to death with that five hundred. It was more cash money than he had ever seen in his life.'

'But you didn't own that piece of property, right?'

'No, so we formed the corporation with a friend in Denver and bought the land from the government. Then we bought four more parcels to throw anyone off the track who found out about it.'

'How did you stop the news of the mineral rights sale from getting to Junction Springs?'

'Our man in Denver scanned every issue of the *Denver Post* and took those sections out of the papers heading for our town that had any story about the mineral rights sale. Not hard to do. He also stopped the bundle of applications going to the county clerk.'

'You owned the copper bearing land, why keep up the idea of stopping me from investigating the whole scheme?'

'The murder of Kramer. That scared

Charest half out of his mind. He hadn't planned it. He just grabbed the gun and shot him before he knew what he was doing. He was after you to stop digging into the killing more than about the land sale.'

'Yes, I understand now. Take your pen and write everything down, just the way it happened. Then we'll take it and go see the sheriff.'

It was just before noon when West walked into the sheriff's office with the mayor. He showed the sheriff the confession and suggested the mayor be held on a kidnapping charge.

Sheriff Ramsden scanned the confession quickly, and then glared at Younger.

'Pelton, how could you get mixed up in something like this? You have enough money. Why?' He took the mayor to a cell and locked him inside.

Back in the front office, Sheriff Ramsden lifted his brows when he looked at West.

'Young man, you do good work. You

just solved a murder for me I'd given up on. Why don't we go give Loophole Charest a visit. Time he lived here in our jail for a while.'

West and the sheriff walked up to the Charest office door and went inside. They found themselves staring into the business end of a double barreled shotgun.

'I saw you taking Younger into the court house, and found out he's been charged,' Charest said. 'So I figured you'd be coming my way soon. Both of you take your weapons out and put them on the desk. Do it right now.'

'Don't make this any worse than it is, Charest,' Sheriff Ramsden said.

'It can't get any worse. Knowing Pelton, he must have talked his head off about everything. No, it can't get any worse. Now both of you down on your faces on the floor. I'm tying you up and gagging you. That way I have a head start.'

'Charest — '

'Shut up, or I'll blast you into the

next county with the double ought buck I have in this Greener.'

They went to the floor and West tried to figure out how to jump Charest. He tied their hands behind their backs first and by then West knew they were beaten, for now.

When both were tied and gagged, Charest sat down and wiped his brow. 'I'm not used to this much work. OK, you're there and I'm leaving. Don't try to follow me. I've had time to get ready. Two hours since I saw West here take Pelton into the court house. I cleaned out my bank account, got all my stocks and bonds in my saddle-bags and I'm ready to move. Don't try to stop me. I'll have a Winchester and a Colt for backup. I've got nothing to lose. You try to stop me and I'll kill you.'

He stood and walked out the back door.

West had been working on the ties on his wrists. It wasn't a good sailor knot. He had it half off five minutes later. Another five minutes and he undid the last knot, turned over, and sat up. He had them both cut loose moments later and ran for the back door.

The only thing he saw there at a tie rail were horse droppings.

'Where would he go?' West asked the sheriff.

'Little town on down the tracks, or he could head north for Denver. Long ride either way.'

'Any way he could get on the train going either direction?' West asked.

'He wouldn't risk getting on here, but I'll check with the train people. They know him. He'd have to buy a ticket.'

'Any sidings where the train stops, say to let a freight or another train go past?'

'Not anywhere down this way that I know of.'

'Mountains. Trains use a lot of water. Any water stops around here anywhere?'

'Yeah. I didn't think of that. About five miles out there's a tank and a water stop. Used to stop for water here in town but it got too messy and the city council asked the railroad to get water somewhere else. The stop is five to seven miles north. What time is it?' He looked at his pocket watch.

'Little after one o'clock. We have the 2.15 leave here and it probably would stop for water. Charest could ride up there and wait for a train going in either direction. I'd think he'd want to get to Denver where he could get lost in the city.'

'I'm riding north,' West said.

'Want me to send a deputy with you?'

'No, just deputize me to keep me legal, and I'll go out and bring him back dead or alive.'

13

West rented a horse from Ihander at the livery and asked if he'd seen lawyer Charest.

'Nope. He has a pair of horses of his own he keeps in back of his place.'

West borrowed a rifle from the stable man and a handful of shells. He loaded it and thanked the man. Then he slid the rifle in the boot of the saddle and headed north. He was taking two calculated risks. First he was assuming that Charest would not try to board the train in Junction Springs. Second he figured he would know all about the train schedule and about the water stop, since he must go to Denver quite often. So he would head for the water stop. He had left soon after one o'clock so he would have plenty of time to ride to the water tower five to seven miles out.

West pushed his mount just a little so she walked at close to five miles an hour. He watched for tracks on the old stage road that led north that was busy before the train came through. Now it was seldom used except for an occasional horseman. He found tracks going north and then lost them. Nothing distinctive about the hoof prints. He found them and lost them for the next hour. He figured he had covered five miles after the hour was up. Now he rode a little quicker, watching ahead, hoping he could see the tower well before he arrived.

The old road had been slanting uphill for the last three miles, now it took a sharper incline. When he rounded a bend next to a creek, he could see the tracks ahead and far in front a water tower with its long swing down arm extended over the tracks. A flume brought water from up the river a ways and spilled it into the tank. He didn't know if anyone watched it or if it just overflowed when the tank filled up.

He kept riding. The only trouble was, Charest should be at the water tower by now. If he was and he looked down the tracks for the coming train, he could see the rider coming.

West turned off into the brush and now lush green forest that grew on the slopes. He'd have to crash brush for the rest of the way and try to be quiet doing it. He went off the trail and across the tracks and the stream to be on the side of the tracks where the water tower sat. Now it was just a matter of moving forward. He figured another mile. When he dismounted and took a look at the tower from the covering brush he saw it was less than a quarter of a mile ahead.

He knew he could move through the trees quieter than the horse could. There was always the chance that one horse would smell the other one and call out a friendly neigh or whinney. He tied the mount to a tree, giving it room enough to do some grazing, then moved forward with his six-gun in hand. He moved steadily ahead. When he figured he was fifty yards from the tower, he edged to the fringe of the brush near the stream and looked north.

He spotted the horse first, tied to a tree twenty yards below the tower in a copse of pine trees. Farther up the hill a bench had been crafted from some logs and limbs. Evidently the trainmen sat there while the engine took on its fill of water for the long steam ahead up the mountains and into Denver.

Sitting there bold as a brass monkey was a man, who could only be Victor Charest. Who else would be out this way waiting for the train?

West had no trouble with the idea of shooting the man without warning. He would have done the same. He cleared a small spot and brought his rifle up. It was about fifty yards, he guessed. He'd shot deer at longer ranges with a rifle. He sighted in on Charest's legs. He refined his sight and squeezed the trigger. Then rammed another round into the chamber and fired again before

Charest had moved. The second shot hit him in the right thigh and the wounded man screamed and tried to stand, but fell. West charged across the distance along the bank of the stream. Charest crawled away but didn't get far.

West put a .45 pistol slug into the ground near his head and he stopped.

'Sonofabitch, you shot me.' He lay on his side. Before West could move, Charest swung out his right hand and fired the pistol he had been hiding. The round hit West in the left shoulder and drove him back a step, but he fired the pistol again hitting Charest in the right shoulder and spinning the weapon out of his hand.

'It's all over, Charest. Give it up. I don't want to kill you right here. A public hanging will be much more satisfying.'

A few minutes later, West had the man tied hand and foot with the rawhide laces from Charest's own boots. Then he found the other man's horse and brought up his own.

'Going for a short ride, Charest. Enjoy it. Be the last outdoors you'll see until the morning of your hanging.'

It took them two hours to ride the six miles back to town. The sheriff took charge of Charest and filled out the paperwork. He was charged with two counts of murder.

* * *

A week later it was all over. West marveled at the swiftness of Western justice. Charest had been charged one day and his trial set for the next day. The trial lasted almost three hours. Two witnesses reported Charest had hired them to kidnap Susan. Mayor Younger testified that Charest had told him that he had killed Kramer in a fit of rage. The all male jury was out for fifteen minutes and came back with a verdict of guilty on all counts. The judge sentenced Charest to be hanged the next day at sunrise. A one trap gallows was built that afternoon.

West had told Charest that he wanted to see him hang. Now he wished that he hadn't. The scene would remain in his mind's eye for many, many years.

Mayor Younger's trial hadn't come up yet. He was playing politics with the sheriff. His charge was conspiracy to commit kidnapping, but because he testified against Charest the penalty would be reduced.

West and Susan had a long talk. She told him she wanted him to come back to Junction Springs after he settled his problem in Boston.

'I want you to be my equal partner in the detective agency,' she said. They sat in the agency after closing for the day. She moved closer to him and reached up and kissed him on the lips. He put his arms around her and returned the kiss. Then he held her tightly in his arms.

'There is so much I want to share with you, David West. Will you come back?'

'Will you wait for me? Promise me

you won't get married to some rich miner or store owner.'

'I promise,' she said. 'I love you, David West. I know it's brazen of me to tell you but ever since you came here — '

He stopped her with another kiss. She pushed hard against his chest and gave a little sigh when the kiss ended.

'Susan Kramer, I don't know who else I'd even think of spending the rest of my life with.' He moved away from her and stood. 'Now, I have twenty minutes to get to the train. I'll wire you every day from Boston and let you know how things are going.'

She started to stand.

'Don't come to the train. I want to remember you right here, the way you look now.' He bent and kissed her once more, then hurried out to the train with his one carpet bag. Deep inside it were Paine's cash and his check and bonds and West's own six-gun and his gunbelt. He might need the Colt in Boston.

14

David West stopped in Denver for three days to buy a new wardrobe. Gone were the denim pants and blue shirts and wide brimmed hat. He settled for a conservative brown suit, two pair of slacks and two shirts, some new underwear and a pair of dress up shoes. He spent the next two days letting his beard grow in. He needed it long enough to change his appearance before he hit Boston. He had two relaxing days of fine dining and a wonderful bed. All the time he was trying to figure out who might have killed Jane Poindexter. On the fourth day he put on his new clothes and bought a ticket on the next train headed east. He had no idea how long it would take him to get to Boston.

He stopped in New York City for a week to let his beard grow. He had started it the day he brought Charest back on the train and turned him over to the sheriff. A full beard and moustache would help him conceal his identity. He also picked up a set of horn-rimmed spectacles with plain glass in the lens, and a hat that he could pull down and cover part of his face.

He arrived at the Boston train station Monday afternoon. He knew he couldn't go to his parents' home or to his old apartment. Instead he found a cheap furnished room in the less desirable part of town and paid for a week in advance. He had thought about how he would go about proving who had killed Jane Poindexter. He had worked over a notebook for days on the train. What he had was a rough outline of how he would do the investigation. He was sure the police had not done anything more once he escaped from them. They knew they had the killer so why look any further?

Money was no problem. He still had most of what he had left with from

Boston including the bearer bonds. The bonds were just like cash, anyone could cash them. Would they be safer in his rented room, or should he open a bank account under the David West name? He decided to leave them in the carpet bag along with Paine's money.

The first day in Boston he went to the *Boston Morning Journal* and asked the librarian there about news stories concerning Jane Poindexter's death. He was showed the files that had the first story and the follow up ones. They covered three weeks, then the story dropped out of the paper.

He read each article in order, scowling at the part about him and his picture, and how he was charged and then escaped from the police. They continued to hunt him.

He had hoped for some new lead, some new angle as to who the killer might have been. A handyman, a merchant, a delivery man, anyone who knew Jane and lusted after her. Now he had a new woman in his life who he had grown to adore and to love in a short two months.

With that nagging doubt erased, he concentrated on what to do next. He had three suspects. J. Thurston Paine was one of them. He wondered if the man had made it back to Boston yet. Just for fun he found a public telephone and called Paine's home number. His mother answered and said that J. Thurston wasn't home right then, but he would be back in two or three hours. He thanked her and hung up. So, he made it home. West had a feeling he would find a way.

The more he thought about Paine, the more he figured that he must be the killer. Why would he get so worked up and go on a wild chase to Colorado? He wanted to be sure that David Johnson was convicted of the crime. So he would concentrate on Paine and ignore for now the other two young men who had tried to dance with Jane.

West checked his beard. It was covering his face nicely. It had nearly three weeks' growth and his moustache was heavy. With the horn-rimmed glasses and the hat, he was sure that no one would recognize him. He went to one of the shops that specialized in clothes for the college crowd and bought two sets that would peg him as either a college student or a newly graduated one.

He had worked out a perfect cover for his investigation. He would be a writer working on a magazine story on Boston's idle rich young people in the 18-22 two year range.

That afternoon West sent a telegram to Susan in Junction Springs. 'Miss you already. Working slowly on my problem here. I'll keep in touch.' He signed it: West.

15

David West sat in a small cafe in downtown Boston and looked over the pocket notebook where he had worked out his strategy for finding Jane's killer. He had several lines to follow. But the best by far looked to be J. Thurston Paine.

He was a real pain but every society matron with any eligible girls invited him to their dinners, dances and parties. They enjoyed seeing what flamboyant outfit he would design for his next performance. West shook his head. At first evaluation, Paine seemed simply too stupid and inefficient and weird to have had the ability and the nerve to attack Jane and strangle her. But he had gone on that wild trip to hunt down the man he thought killed Jane. That made him the best suspect for Jane's death. He went to the telegraph office and sent a wire to Susan in Colorado.

'Having a dull working time. Wish you were here. I'd show you Boston. Maybe next year. Still struggling to come up with the man who killed Jane. I'll keep you informed. Love you. West.'

He sent it, not even noticing how much it cost, then went back to his room and tried to figure out how to check up on Paine.

The next morning he was on a telephone at a nearby hotel. He couldn't go to officials or records, so he went to his network of young Bostonians who ran in the same circle that Paine did. Some of them he knew well and he would have to disguise his voice. He started with Mary Steward, who was twenty, home from college, Vassar he thought, and a delight at any party or dance. He used the magazine interview gambit and it worked.

'Oh, yes, I'd be delighted to talk to you about Boston society and the younger set. We have a darling time. It's not all fun and frolic either. I'm on three charity committees, and my mother is putting me on another. Yes, I love college. Vassar is so impressive, so . . . so educational. That sounds strange, but I'm learning so much. Now about the parties. The biggest one is The Charity Ball. We had it a few months ago and a tragedy. A girl was murdered who had been at the ball. But then you know about that.'

'What's the thinking by the social set? Did someone who was at the ball do the crime?'

'I had never thought about that. I know one of the boys there was arrested, but he got away from the police. I don't think I've heard anything about it lately.'

'If you had to pick someone from the ball who did the dastardly deed, who would you pick?'

The line went dead for a moment.

'Oh, dear. I don't know if I could. Well, let's see. One boy did get in trouble a year ago, but I think his parents bought off the girl and sent the son to work in the family's British company. Not him.'

'I've been getting some bad stories about a man called J. Thurston Paine. Do you think he could have had anything to do with Jane's death?'

'Oh, my. I had been thinking about Mr Paine. He does have a bad reputation, but most think that's because of the wild way he always dresses. A real fop, a clown. But murder? I don't know. Somehow he looks like a harmless fool. Yet you never know. An idea. Do you know Mrs Wayland Anderson? She knows everyone who is anyone in Boston. I'm sure she can give you some information about Mr Paine.'

He thanked her and hung up. It took him another day to track down Mrs Wayland Anderson. They were old money, banking mostly, and they had been in Europe on vacation but were just back. She was home now and busy with her charity projects. He wrangled an appointment with her the following afternoon for tea at three o'clock.

A butler opened the ten foot high front door and showed him into the library where an elegant woman in her sixties smiled up at him over a sterling silver tea service.

'You would be Mr West. Do sit down. I'm Sylvia Anderson. Could I pour you some tea?'

They chatted about the weather and then about the state of society today in Boston. She was concerned because those who could afford it were simply not contributing enough to the cultural projects of the city.

He explained what he was doing with the article and promised that he would list all of the charity programs that the people in his article worked on. He slid around some names and then brought up Paine.

Mrs Anderson made a sour face. 'I really would appreciate it if you could do your article without mentioning Mr Paine. He has been a strange person lately. Even though his family is well thought of he is something of a clown.'

'Oh, he seemed charming when I talked to him. Has he been in trouble with the law, or with any of the parents of the young ladies in the social whirl?'

Mrs Anderson frowned. 'Yes and no. I've had three or four mothers talk to me in hushed tones about what their daughters told them about Mr Paine. He had gone on a rampage, quietly of course, and tried to seduce three young ladies at three different parties. He was unsuccessful, but it just goes to show you the kind of person he is.

'Most of us still wonder about something that happened ten years ago. My best friend's daughter told her mother about it. You may remember the case. One of our groups had a picnic in the park with refreshments and games. Some of the younger boys and girls ventured into the woods playing hide and seek.

'The upshot of it was that one of the 14-year-old girls was found strangled in the park. There were ten or fifteen girls and about that many boys in the woods at the time, but there never were any charges brought against anyone.

'However, my best friend's daughter later dated J. Thurston Paine for a while when she was eighteen. They talked about that time ten years before. Melinda told her mother that Paine seemed to know too much about the murder scene. He described it to her in livid detail. Then said that he had happened by it when the police were there before they ran him off.'

'Was Paine ever questioned by the police about it, recently I mean?'

'Not that I know of. But Melinda told her mother that she was almost certain that J. Thurston had killed the girl.'

'Can you tell me anyone else who has been dating Mr Paine, recently?'

'Let me see. Most of the youngsters get away from me. I'll have to ask Melinda. Could you call me tomorrow about this time? I'll be busy in the morning, but I'll be home then.'

West said he could and walked out of the house with a new interest in J. Thurston Paine.

He sent his daily telegram to Susan, and then had a big dinner at one of the better restaurants. He tensed when two couples he knew well came in and walked past his table. He had taken his hat off and had to trust on his beard and the glasses. The women glanced at him and then looked away without the least bit of recognition. He took a deep breath and finished his dessert.

The next afternoon he called on the phone and Mrs Anderson told him one girl had dated Paine three times before she broke it off. Her name was Genevieve Flowers. She also gave him the girl's phone number.

He made the call at once. She wasn't home. Her mother said she would be home after six o'clock. She was working in a food store handing out packages of food to the poor.

He called her on the phone and she

at first didn't want to talk about Paine.

'Yes, I went out with him three times. But I'll never see him again. He's no gentleman, that's all I have to say.'

'Have you heard that he may have had something to do with that 14-year-old girl who was killed ten years ago in that picnic in the park?'

'Oh my, that's coming up again. He mentioned it and said he thought it had all died down. Then he got abusive. He actually tore my blouse one night and I had to kick him and scream and then run away from him. We were in our back yard garden here at home, or I would have been in big trouble. I told my father and he took his shotgun outside, but Paine had left by then.' She shivered just remembering the night.

'Oh my, I don't know why I'm telling you all this.'

'It might help catch a killer. Do you think that Paine could have had anything to do with the death of Jane Poindexter three months ago?'

He heard only a sudden gasp of breath.

'Oh, goodness, he was there that night. He tried to dance with Jane, I saw him talking to her. But she turned him down. He could have been angry enough. I just don't know. He could have. He likes to get rough with girls.'

He thanked her and hung up the phone. Thank you, Mr Alexander Graham Bell for your invention of the telephone. It may have helped him find Jane's killer.

16

West thought it through. Paine could be the killer. He knew that Jane left with him that night after the ball. He could have gone to Jane's house and hidden across the street and waited for West to bring her home. Then he saw her kiss him twice, and that must have infuriated him. So he slipped around to her window, and rapped on it. She opened it and he surprised her and charged into the room grabbing her mouth so she couldn't scream.

What did he know about Paine? He worked in his father's law firm. Paine had never been to law school, so West had no idea what he did at the office. He had to follow Paine for a while and see what he did. It took him two days to find Paine when he came out of the law offices about noon. He went to lunch with a surprisingly pretty woman, then took her back to the firm and stepped into a cab. West caught a one horse cab and followed him. Paine wound up in the outskirts of Boston at a tavern with a shady reputation.

Inside West had a beer at the bar and checked around. Paine was no where in sight. He talked to the barkeep.

'Hey, I was supposed to meet my buddy, J. Thurston Paine here for a beer. Has he come in yet?'

West had abandoned his college crowd type clothes and wore a regular Boston business suit. The bar apron scowled for a minute.

'Yeah, he's here. Didn't even ask about you, just went to the back room. Gonna be a big doings back there today. Cost half the farm to buy in.'

'Rats, I didn't bring any cash with me. Guess I'll have to catch him the next time.'

That afternoon West wrote Paine a letter on plain white paper. The letter said: 'J. Thurston Paine. I know that you killed Jane Poindexter. I also know that you killed that girl in the park ten years ago. I will be quiet and not go to the police if you bring ten thousand dollars to the park on Elmont Street tomorrow, the 16th at 7 p.m. Place it in a plain paper sack and leave it on the park bench near the statue of George Washington. If the money is not there, I will take my evidence to the police. It is convincing, and will convict you of Jane's murder. Then you'll hang. Be sure to have the money there, and no tricks.'

He didn't sign the letter. The next morning he went to the law offices and paid a small boy fifty cents to take the letter to the receptionist in the lobby. It had Paine's name on the outside and was marked 'personal'. The young boy was delighted. Paine faded out the door just as the boy handed the letter over. He turned to point where West had been when he talked to the man. He was no longer there.

West kept away from the Paine law firm building. He sent a wire to Susan, and then checked out the Elmont Street Park. He'd been there dozens of times. He went to the bench and looked at the statue, then moved away from it to find a good spot where he could hide and watch the delivery, if it ever came. He wasn't interested in the money, but if Paine came it would mean he was guilty.

He had a big supper that night and got to the park an hour early. He hid in his spot and waited. Ten minutes later a man came who could be Paine. He was with two men who carried long cardboard boxes. Paine looked around the area and found hiding spots for each man. Once they were in position, West saw them take rifles out of the boxes and sight in on the bench. Then Paine went away.

He came back five minutes until seven. This time he carried a brown paper bag. He put it on the bench, walked around it twice, then shrugged and hurried away. West watched the spots where the two men were hidden.

Neither of them moved for a half hour. It was getting dark. One man came out of the hiding spot with his rifle in the box, went to the bench and picked up the paper sack and walked away.

West faded into the darkness as well in the other direction. In his hotel room he wrote another letter.

'Mr Paine, shame on you trying to kill me with hidden riflemen. You should know better. Your little mistake cost you another ten thousand dollars. Bring twenty thousand dollars in bills to the Riverside Park off Sixtieth Street at 6 p.m. today. There is a picnic table close to the water. Leave a carpet bag there with the twenty thousand in it. Any tricks this time and I'll hunt you down and kill you myself. Enjoy the rest of your day.'

The next day West arrived at the park early just before five o'clock. A family of four had just finished an afternoon picnic and left the table closest to the water and walked back to their buggy. He had a pair of binoculars and hid in some trees a short way from the picnic table. For ten minutes he scanned the expanse of the park. Here it was almost flat and he could see for a quarter of a mile in three directions with the water in the fourth. He saw no buggies in the parking area, no lingering men, and nothing that looked dangerous. He settled down to wait.

It was fifteen minutes before six when a buggy pulled into the parking area near the picnic tables. A man stepped down who could be Paine, and he carried a small carpet bag. So far, so good. By trying to bushwhack him yesterday, Paine had all but admitted that he had killed Jane. What would he try this time?

Paine looked around, spotted the table and walked to it and sat down staring out at the water.

West waited. It was ten minutes after six before he stepped out of the trees and walked quickly toward the table. Paine heard him coming and turned. West pulled his Colt from where he had stuffed it in his belt and covered the foppish man.

'Easy, Paine, don't get in trouble now. Open the bag and show me the bills.'

Paine stared at him from ten feet away. 'I should know you. That voice. The beard could be a cover-up. Yes! You have to be Douglas Johnson. I'll have the police on you within twelve hours.'

'Why do you think you'll live that long?' West asked. 'Stand away from the money, and then get down on your belly on the ground. Down, now.'

Paine hesitated. West waved the six-gun at him and he dropped.

West heard them before he saw them. Hoof beats. He looked up and saw two riders coming over a slight rise from the north. They both had rifles and were galloping hard directly at him.

When they were at fifty yards, West fired his pistol at them as a warning. One of the riflemen fired his weapon, but the hard riding horse caused the round to go twenty feet over West's head. The riders came closer. At thirty yards, Paine fired two shots. One of the horses bleated in pain and shied to one side. The other rider kept coming, his rifle up. West fired again, then a fifth time. The gunman on the horse was less than twenty yards away when the last slug zinged past his head. His eyes went wide and he whirled his mount and charged away, chasing the first rider who was almost over the rise.

West looked back at Paine. He had stood and had taken two steps toward the buggy when West stopped him.

'I've still got one round, Paine. Where do you want me to shoot you?'

Paine turned. 'Johnson, you wouldn't do that. You're not a killer.'

'Ask three men out in Colorado that who are right now moldering in their graves. Back to the table and sit.'

West went to the table and opened the carpet bag. It contained only three folded newspapers.

'Stand up,' West told Paine. When the

man had fully stood, West had transferred his Colt into his left hand and pounded his hard fist solidly into Paine's nose. Blood spurted. Paine screamed. He held his bloody nose with his hand.

'Now get out of here before I put a bullet in your head. I'm turning my evidence over to the police tomorrow afternoon.'

He watched Paine walk slowly toward his buggy. Then when he must have figured he was out of pistol range, he looked back, and ran for the rig.

Driving back to town in his own rented buggy, West worked on what to do next.

* * *

That evening West moved to a better hotel and used a different name when he registered. Then he telephoned his father at his home.

'Father, it's me, Douglas.' There was a long pause.

'Where are you, Douglas?'

'I'm here in town, Dad, I know who killed Jane Poindexter, but I can't quite prove it. It was J. Thurston Paine. Don't tell the police that I'm here. I need another day or two to tie up Paine for the police.'

'Where have you been?'

'Out in Colorado. But that can wait. I just wanted you to know that I didn't hurt Jane, and that I'm almost ready to bring the killer to justice. I'll keep you informed.'

'We knew you didn't do it, but all that evidence — '

'Circumstantial and not the right evidence. You'll see. Tell Mother that I'm fine.'

'Good to hear from you. Be careful. If he killed once, he might again.'

'I'll be careful.'

* * *

The next morning West sat in a doorway three houses down from

Paine's apartment. He was out of sight but could see the door to the apartment easily. An hour later, just after seven o'clock, Paine left and hurried down the street where he could catch a cab.

West waited until he was out of sight, and then walked up to the door. He took out a ring of keys he had obtained that afternoon, and soon found one to fit the lock. It opened and he was inside. He paused a moment, letting his eyes adjust to the dim light. Then he began a systematic search of the place. Nothing in the small kitchen or the living room. The one bedroom was different.

On a bulletin board propped up on the dresser were dozens of newspaper clippings and pictures. He recognized at once that many of them were of Jane Poindexter.

He looked closer in the dresser, behind it, and in the closet. In the bottom drawer of a small desk he found a large scrap-book. Inside were more clippings and stories. Several pages were given to Jane's death. One item taped in the book was the dance program that Jane had used the night she was killed. Another was a blue ribbon that had been in her hair that night.

Then he found several pages of clippings about the 14-year-old girl who had been killed ten years before. The stories said that certain items belonging to the girl had been taken from her body. They included a locket, a dance program with her name on it, and several photos of her and friends. He found all three items in the scrapbook.

He had it. He had enough to convince any jury that Paine had killed both the young girl and Jane Poindexter. He closed the scrapbook and put it under his arm, then tried to get everything else back the way it had been when he arrived. He was just ready to go out the front door, when he heard a key turning in the lock.

There was no place to hide as the door opened and J. Thurston Paine stared at David West from three feet away.

17

West knew someone was coming in. Paine had no idea anyone was inside. That gave West a great advantage of striking first. West charged forward like a bull, smashing into Paine, slamming him out the door onto the small porch, dumping him on his back as West raced down the street, the treasured scrap-book firmly under his right arm and held with his hand.

He ran for three blocks, and then wheezed to a stop. He was out of condition. He gasped for breath as he looked behind. Paine had not followed him. He walked rapidly for three more blocks before he found a place where he could get a cab, and then rode quickly back to his new hotel. He hurried upstairs to the second floor and used his key to room 204, closed the door and dropped on the bed, exhausted.

He stared at the ceiling. He had it. He had all of the evidence a good prosecuting attorney would need to convict Paine. For a second a phrase slashed into his joy. Search warrant. He had no warrant to search Paine's apartment. The whole case could get thrown out of court. He didn't know much about the law, but the warrant was one thing he did know. He shrugged. A good prosecutor would find a way to get the clippings and the mementos of the killings introduced. Maybe they could still get a warrant and find the other clippings on the wall in Paine's apartment. He must have lots of them there.

West went out for supper and then phoned his father.

'I've got the evidence we need,' he said. Then he explained what he had and his father groaned. They talked about the problem of a search warrant.

'There must be other evidence. What about fingerprints at the scene that they didn't identify? Do they still have them?'

His father didn't know.

'Why don't you bring the scrapbook to the office tomorrow morning and we'll look it over and talk about it. No police will be here. We'll see what we can figure out then.'

They hung up and West went back to his hotel. He slept better that night than he had in two weeks.

The next morning West took the scrapbook, wrapped it in heavy paper, put it in a big paper sack and headed for his father's stocks and bonds office in the Johnson Securities building. It was good to be back in the familiar surroundings. The moment he walked into his father's office he knew there was trouble. A man he wasn't sure he recognized stood looking out the window.

West and his father shook hands. Then they all sat down.

'Douglas, this is Mr Martin Poindexter, Jane's father.'

'Mr Poindexter, I'm so sorry about what happened.'

The man's expression was strained, and West had the impression he was holding back his true feelings. He nodded.

Mr Johnson pointed at the package West carried.

'Is that the scrapbook?'

'Yes.'

'Douglas, we have a new problem. Sometime last night Mr Poindexter's daughter, Jennifer, was kidnapped right out of her room. The kidnapper left a note on her pillow.' He handed West a piece of paper.

'To a thief: I demand that a certain scrapbook be returned to its rightful owner today at high noon in Franklin Park near the fountain. Jennifer will be sent home as soon as the scrapbook is turned over and no police are present. There is no room for discussion or compromise. If the item is not brought back the fate of Miss Poindexter will be on your head. Be there at noon today.'

West looked at Mr Poindexter. 'Of course I'll take it back. Even convicting this criminal of murder isn't worth endangering Jennifer. But I'll have to do it alone. If anyone else is there, he simply won't show up.'

'We've talked about that and agree,' Mr Johnson said. 'You'll be alone. Deliver the package and then we'll see where we are about charging Paine with the death of Jane.'

West stood and paced the big office. 'I wonder about getting another scrap-book that looks like this one and delivering it instead of the real one. No, he would know in an instant it was a fake and even if I captured him, he would never tell me where he held Jennifer. I can give the scrapbook back and then we could put some Pinkerton detectives to watch his house. We could get a warrant today and have it ready, so as soon as he takes the scrapbook back to his apartment we will raid the place.'

'First we have to give it back to him,' Mr Johnson said. 'After that we'll see what we have to do.'

'Could I see the scrapbook?' Mr Poindexter asked.

'Yes, of course.' West unwrapped it and handed it to Jane's father. He opened it and found the place where Jane's pictures were and the dance program and her hair ribbon. Tears seeped out of his eyes and he brushed them away. He closed the book quickly and handed it back to West.

'Yes, there is no doubt. J. Thurston Paine must have killed my Jane.' He looked at West. 'When you deliver it, don't you think you should be armed?'

West grinned and flipped back his suit jacket to show the Colt six-gun pushed under his belt. 'I think this will take care of any shooting I need to do.'

Mr Poindexter was surprised.

'I've been out West, sir. Out in Colorado. A man has to have a gun there sometimes to protect himself. I won't use it unless I have to. I want to see this animal tried and hung.'

* * *

West went to the park, arriving there at 11.30. He checked out the bench near the fountain. It was in an open area, with trees and shrubs back fifty feet or so all around it and the fountain. Two gardeners trimmed some shrubs on one side of the area. He sat on the bench for a while, then walked away with the scrapbook. He timed it so he returned two minutes until noon. He put the package wrapped securely again, on the bench beside him. He looked around, then stood and walked away leaving the scrapbook. He was twenty feet away when he saw an elderly woman with a cane coming toward the bench. He looked past her, hunting Paine. Nobody else was in the park. The old woman sat down on the bench, noticed the package and looked around. Then she cut open the wrappings with a knife and looked inside.

West was about to run back and tell the woman to leave the package there, when the old woman stood. She dropped the cane, held the scrapbook tightly under her right arm and ran like a sprinter for the woods and brush just down the hill.

It wasn't an old woman. The figure ran like a man. It had to be Paine. West whirled and raced after the person with the scrapbook. Paine entered the woods, and West heard someone shout, but he kept running. He hit the woods and could hear Paine ahead of him. The section of woodland was only a half block wide here and ended in city streets and houses. He had to catch Paine before he left the woods. He heard more shouts from the sides, but charged ahead. Twice he saw Paine who had discarded the dress and hat and wore gray pants and a blue shirt. He looked back at West and screamed at him, then vanished down the side of the hill through some thick brush. West came closer and pulled out his six-gun and fired a warning shot. That brought more shouts from behind him.

He cleared the brush and found Paine bent over, panting thirty feet ahead. West leveled in with the six-inch barreled Colt and fired four times. One of the rounds hit Paine in the thigh and knocked him down. He jumped up, and tried to run, but fell again. He pushed up and limped toward the street.

Ten long strides later and West tackled Paine from behind and drove him into the mulch under the scattering of trees. He sat on Paine's back and listened to him wail. Paine still clutched the scrapbook.

Moments later ten men in all kind of clothes including the two gardeners surrounded them. Mr Johnson hurried up.

'Good, you got him. These men are policemen. We call them undercover in their civilian clothes. I wasn't going to let you go after Paine alone.'

West rolled Paine over. 'Where is Jennifer?' he asked.

Paine laughed at him. 'You'll never find her now.'

Another man raced up out of breath, carrying a small hand gun. It was Mr

Poindexter. As soon as he came up to Paine, he fired a round into the dirt beside his head.

He knelt and put the pistol muzzle against Paine's forehead.

'Now, Mr Paine. You will tell me where Jennifer is, or you will be shoveling coal for the devil within two minutes.'

A police lieutenant hurried up and took the weapon away from Mr Poindexter.

'Sir, I'm Lieutenant Wilson, of the Boston police. Your daughter is in the park somewhere. I have twenty men searching right now. We saw him bring her in, but then lost her. We couldn't get too close to him. We'll find her. I'll take over now.' He pulled the scrapbook from Paine.

He stood Paine up and led him hobbling toward the street and a police carriage. He watched West who paced them.

'You must be Douglas Johnson,' the lieutenant said. 'Searched this town upside down for you couple of months ago. We'll put Paine in the wagon with guards and then go back and we'll all look for Jennifer.'

They found her a half hour later wearing her nightgown and sitting on a blanket under a tree inside of some thick brush. She was tied hand and foot and had a gag but was unhurt. Her father untied her and took out the gag and she hugged him and cried and he carried her out to the street where they got in a cab.

* * *

On the way back to the Johnson Securities office, West's father told him what else he had done.

'This morning we got a search warrant for Paine's apartment. The police will go in now that they have Paine. Also I talked with our lawyer. He handles a lot of criminal cases. He said giving the scrapbook back to Paine was a good idea. Then when we captured him with it on his person, we would be free to use anything in it as evidence to convict him. It doesn't matter where the book had been before then, or how he came to lose it. The fact that it was in his possession makes it fair game as evidence for the prosecution.'

West gave a big sigh. 'I hadn't thought that far ahead. Now I'm sure that there won't be any trouble getting a conviction. He might be tried for the death of that little girl ten years ago, too. Are his connections good enough that he can escape the hangman's noose for both crimes?'

'Not sure. That will have to be up to the courts.'

At the office he asked if he could telephone in a telegram to the local office.

'Yes, we do it all the time now. Go right ahead.'

He wrote out the message. 'Susan. I miss you. I want to come back to Junction Springs as soon as I can. Some minor clean up to do here. I found the man who killed Jane, and that's all taken care of. You can send me a wire back to Johnson Securities, 1212 Embassy Street. Boston. Miss you. Love you. David West.'

He sent the wire, and then his father came into West's office. It was exactly the way he had left it.

'I've been thinking about the West. That's where the big push is going to be. Things are booming out that way. Denver is growing like a spring colt. I'm wondering if you'd like to set up a branch of Johnson Securities in Denver?'

'That's a surprise,' West said. 'I didn't know that you had any plans on expanding. I was a detective in Colorado. I thought I might go back to that line of work.'

'Think about it. You're good with people and you understand the market and investments. You could do well in Denver. You think it over and let me know.'

'I'll do that. First I better go turn

myself in down at police headquarters. As far as I know I'm still a wanted outlaw.'

He walked into the Boston police building and approached a sergeant at a high desk.

'Sergeant, I'm turning myself in. My name is Douglas Johnson, and I'm wanted for murder.'

The sergeant looked at him severely. Then he nodded. 'Oh, yes, Mr Johnson. Indeed you were on our list of wanted men, but magically your name was erased from it just an hour ago. Lieutenant Wilson himself came down and withdrew the warrant and told me if you showed up to ask you to go see him. He's on the second floor.' He looked around and spotted a uniformed officer.

'Bolt, take this gentleman up to see Lieutenant Wilson. We don't want him to get lost'

In the office, Wilson shook West's hand. 'Want to thank you for your work on the Poindexter case. It had us completely baffled. Paine must have slipped in just the way we figured, surprised her and maybe knocked her out before he killed her. At least we have everything we need for a speedy trial. I know his family is well situated but money can't beat this one. He might get it knocked down to life in prison but he won't ever molest any more young ladies.'

'Good. Now I've got some things to clean up. I'll be going back to Colorado. I like it out there.'

'One other thing, that weapon you used with the long barrel, is that what they call a six-gun out West?'

'That's it.'

'Do you have it with you? I'd like to take a look at it.'

'Sorry, I left it in my office. You can buy one from the *Sears and Roebuck* catalog. Well, I better be getting back. Thanks for taking me off the Most Wanted list of criminals.'

'My pleasure.' He frowned. 'Colorado. The trial won't be coming up for several months if I know lawyers. But then I don't think we'll need your testimony. No, the district attorney should have plenty. You have a good trip.'

Just as West returned to the Johnson Securities offices, he saw a telegram delivery boy coming out. Up in his office his father tapped an envelope on his desk.

'Doug, you have a telegram.'

He grabbed it and went into his office. It could only be from Susan. No one else would send him a wire. He tore open the envelope and read the message.

'Glad you're about done there. Looking forward to seeing you again. Actually I can't wait, but I guess I have to. Your Susan.'

18

It took West two days to close up his apartment, sell some of his furniture, and give the rest to charity. He packed two large carpet bags and one trunk with his clothes and things he couldn't part with, then had a conference with his barber, a man he had known for ten years.

'Yes, it's me, Douglas, Mr Warnick. Want you to chop off this beard with your clippers, and then shave me down to my bare skin. Take it all off, the beard and mustache.'

The deed was done in twenty minutes and Douglas felt more like himself. Then he had a conference with his father.

'I sent a man to Denver yesterday to shop around for a proper office for our branch in that city. Johnson Securities, Inc, Denver, will have to be registered with the state and all of that. Our lawyer will be out there in three days to handle those matters.'

'Things will be slow to start,' West said. 'The branch will lose money for the first year, at least. Can we handle that?'

'Absolutely. I was figuring maybe two years before we showed a profit out there. You'll have to start with one office girl and yourself. We have two customers I know of in Colorado, and I'll suggest that they shift their accounts to you there in Denver. We'll work it out.'

'I've put my savings and checking accounts together here and I'll be transferring that balance to Denver as soon as I decide on a bank there. First I'll go to Junction Springs and take care of some important business.'

'That would be Susan. I heard you send your telegram yesterday. Then that one you received you showed me. Whenever you're ready we'll get things started. Will Susan be moving to

Denver as well?'

'That is a good question. I'll have to ask her. But I think I can talk her into it.'

* * *

Four days later, David West walked into the Kramer Detective Agency and surprised Susan.

'Oh, David. I'm so glad to see you.' She ran and threw her arms around him and kissed him. After a long embrace and several more kisses they sat close together on the small sofa that faced her desk.

'So much to tell you I don't know where to start. But I want to take you out to lunch, or dinner, if you want to call it that. How about right now?'

Over their apple pie dessert, he asked her how Rocky was doing.

'He's as feisty as ever. Was in the office almost all day yesterday asking me about you.'

'Good, I'll go see him today. First,

there's something we need to talk about.'

'You look serious.'

'I am serious. Are we engaged? Did I ever ask you to marry me, or did I just assume that you would?'

Her eyes went wide, a smile broke on her face, and she reached across the table and kissed him.

A woman in the booth across from them shook her head in disapproval. 'You young people these days. When I was your age — '

Susan cut her off. 'Mrs Partridge, I just got engaged. This is David West, my fiancé.'

The woman smiled. 'Yes dear, then I guess it's all right. This time.'

Susan reached across the table and caught both of his hands.

'Yes, of course I'll marry you.' She squealed and everyone looked at her. She covered her face that was glowing a light pink. 'Well, I couldn't help it. I've never been engaged before.' Her face sparkled with a happiness he could only imagine.

'Wow. Golly. I'm really engaged to be married.'

'No ring. I'll have to get you one.'

'Doesn't matter, right now I'm floating on a cloud, so girlish and giggly I could burst.'

He held her hands tightly. 'I'll keep you from floating away anywhere. We can't have an engaged woman like you floating around town without touching the ground.'

'I think I might just do that.' She took a deep breath. 'Now tonight we will grab a chicken from the butcher, no, let's get a couple of inch thick steaks and we'll have a real big supper at my house.'

'Agreed. Now are you settled down enough that we can walk back to the office? I want to kiss you a few times in private.'

'A few times.' She giggled. 'How about a few hundred?' She laughed. 'Now that was naughty of me. I'm no good to do anything at the office for the rest of the day. You walk me home and I'll start getting a candlelight dinner ready for you. First the butcher.'

A short time later he left her at her house after a lingering kiss at the front door. He'd never seen her so happy.

Tuesday morning West had Dr Eaton check his two gunshot wounds, treat and rebandage them. They were starting to heal, but he still couldn't use his left arm for much. Then he had the next serious talk with Susan.

He poured her a fresh cup of coffee and settled into the chair across from her desk.

'This looks important,' she said.

'Gave myself away.' He sipped at his coffee. 'How would you like to move the Kramer Detective Agency to Denver?'

'Denver,' she was caught by total surprise. Her eyes went wide and she cocked her head to one side. 'Now why on earth would I want to move my business to Denver?'

'Not much business in this town. You're not getting rich. Barely keep the office open some months, Rocky tells me. Why not Denver?'

'Because it's a big city. It's noisy and dirty and there are so many people there that I'd get a headache just walking to work.'

'Or riding the streetcar.'

'They have streetcars there?'

'Probably. Denver is growing fast. It's going to be the hub of the West for a long time. A jumping off place. Lots of big money is there and more going in every day. Room for a good detective agency.'

She frowned, took a sip of her coffee and stared at him over the cup. 'We're still engaged even if I don't want to go to Denver?'

'Yes, we're still engaged.'

'Well, give me three more good reasons I should pick up and move. Land sakes, I've never lived anywhere but Junction City in my entire life.'

'A good business opportunity.'

'You really think that we should move our business to Denver? Remember we are an equal partnership now, fifty-fifty right down the ledger sheet.'

'I never really agreed to that as I remember. But there is one more factor I haven't told you. Johnson Securities Inc. is going to open a branch office in Denver. My legal name is Douglas Johnson and the security company is owned by my family. My father wants me to go to Denver and open our branch office there. I'd be the manager and only employee for a while.'

'Wow, you really know how to confuse a girl. Engaged, I figured we'd get married here and both work in the agency here and eventually you could run it on your own and I'd stay home and raise a flock of kids and bake you cherry pies.'

'Still could work out almost that way.'

'But when we get married, you'd be in Denver at some big company and I'd be here running the agency . . . no that won't work.'

'So what will work?'

'You're set on opening the securities

business in Denver?'

'Yes, it's already underway. Our lawyer will be there tomorrow.'

'And we're still going to get married?'

'If you'll still have me.'

'I most certain will still have you. And you and I still have Kramer Detective Agency?'

'About the size of it.'

'Won't work.'

He frowned. 'What do you mean it won't work?'

'We can't be married and keep the detective agency here in Junction Springs.'

'So then — '

'So then we'll just close up the agency. The only reason I took it over is because I couldn't sell it to anyone in town. There were a few clients to finish working with. Tomorrow we close the doors and I'll stay home and plan our wedding. When is it going to be?'

West jumped up, his face a series of smiles. 'Hooray! The problem is solved. You'll come to Denver with me as a bride and a housewife and won't have to worry about being a detective.'

'Like I said, I never was crazy about being a detective anyway. Now, when are we getting married?'

'Whenever you say. You work out the time and the details. A week, two weeks, three weeks. We get married here in the church and then take off on the train for Denver. Before then you can come to Denver and we'll pick out a house to buy or rent. I want you to be happy with our new home.'

She came around the desk, pushed him down on the sofa, and sat on his lap. After one long kiss, she cuddled against him.

'I don't think in my entire life that I've been happier. I'm closing up the office here right now.' She jumped up and skipped to the door, pushed on the locks and pulled down the shade.

'Now, the Kramer Detective Agency is officially closed and out of business. Where were we?'

Other titles in the
Linford Western Library:

DEATH ON THE DEVIL'S HIGHWAY

Josh Lockwood

Innocent, yet sentenced to hang for a murder, mustang man Auggie Kellerman escapes from custody hoping to clear his name. But now he's fair game for every lawman, bounty hunter, and Indian-tracker in the Arizona Territory. He's also a target for the 'Copper King', Charlie Keogh, who stands to lose everything if he makes it back alive. Now, he must ride the Devil's Highway, a harsh and dangerous trail — and administer some six-gun justice to save his reputation.

THE HELLRAKERS

Owen G. Irons

Meeting Van Connely and his gang is like coming face to face with hell . . . Skyler Lynch has hired the men, along with his friend Randy Staggs, to drive his horses southward to the Pocono country, where he and his daughter Kate have a ranch. But Connely steals the herd and murders Lynch before going on a rampage across the Southwest. Randy Staggs, left alive, vows to track him down, to the ends of the earth if necessary . . .

SABINAS KID

Steve Ritchie

After receiving a four-month-old letter from his mother in which she asks for his help, Caleb McConnell heads home to Colorado. But along the trail an attempt is made on his life, and Caleb begins to understand something of his parents' troubles. Why is someone after his folks' ranch, and who is behind it? When Caleb finally reaches Del Norte, childhood friendships are renewed, old grudges re-hashed, and guns blaze across the Rio Grande Valley as the mystery unfolds.